Sir William Bowlinggreen
and Company

Sir William Bowlinggreen and Company

By DC Fidler

DCFidler Publishing
2018

Published by DCFidler Publishing
1117 University Avenue, #505
Morgantown, WV 26505
DCFidlerpublishing@gmail.com

Printed in the United States of America
by Lulu Press, Inc.

This play is entirely a work of fiction.
Any resemblance to actual persons, living or dead,
is entirely coincidental.

ISBN: 978-1-7327521-0-8
Library of Congress Control Number: 2018910423

Characters

William Bowlinggreen (55) Director, writer, and lead actor

Lillian Bowlinggreen (50) Wife of William, costumer, and lead actress

Betsy Nesbeth (17) Aspiring actress and faithful to the King James Bible

Joshua Parker (17) Aspiring actor, rescued from orphanage by Annie Dumbstrum

Samuel Postwaite (75) Aging supporting actor and stage hand who prefers unadulterated Shakespeare

Margaret Parsons (70) Aging supporting actress, grandmother to Betsy Nesbeth

Annie Dumbstrum (40) Attractive supporting actress, "aunt" to Joshua Parker

Ian Durboville (35) Supporting actor and a mystery

Setting

All action takes place in the late 1890s on American West saloon stages, in various hotel rooms, and by the Arkansas River in Dodge City.

Appreciation

Many phrases are fully or partially quoted from William Shakespeare, Charles Dickens, and other poets' works. Those phrases are set in italics. Since both authors enriched the English language enormously, their phrases and meanings for words are infused throughout daily discourse and writing. Those commonly used words and phrases are not italicized. Plots are deliberately "borrowed," the purpose of this play. I am forever indebted to my daily heroes, Masters Shakespeare and Dickens.

An earlier version of *Sir William Bowlinggreen and Company,* entitled *Master William Bowlinggreen and Company,* premiered at M.T. Pockets Theatre in Morgantown, West Virginia on October 20, 2006.

Cast

William Bowlinggreen	Christian Cox
Lillian Bowlinggreen	Angela Lacey-McCracken
Betsy Nesbeth	Loren Bane
Joshua Parker	Joe Spelman
Samuel Postwaite	Jim Connelly
Margaret Parsons	Charlotte Haas
Annie Dumbstrum	Melissa Ryan
Ian Durboville	Ed French

Staff

Director	Matt Haught
Assistant Director/Stage Manager	
	John Harvey
Production Designer	Dan Stewart
Lighting Design	Bill Blaker
Props Master	Erin Mihalik
Carpenter	Josh Feather

Executive Producer for M.T. Pockets Theatre
Toni Morris
Assistant Producer for M.T. Pockets Theatre
Vicki Trickett

Act One · Scene One

Drum roll.

WILLIAM, wearing black suspenders, steps before the main curtain.

WILLIAM: Good evening ladies and gentlemen of this vast heartland. Welcome to a delightful evening's saloon divertissement, presented for your pleasure by Master William Bollinggreen, yours truly, and Company.

(LILLIAN enters, carrying red suspenders.)

LILLIAN: Those suspenders won't do at'tall, William deary. These pretty ones will.

(LILLIAN hands red suspenders to WILLIAM.)

WILLIAM: Lillian, I wear manly suspenders.
LILLIAN: Exactly, dear, pretty.

(LILLIAN walks toward side stage and stops.)

WILLIAM: Tonight, the year of our Lord, one thousand eight hundred and ninety—
LILLIAN: Oh William?
WILLIAM: Blast it, Lilly. I am preluding.
LILLIAN: How does my toga look?
WILLIAM: Toga-esque as any costume informs.

1

LILLIAN: I hemmed it a bit. It belonged to Nicholas. Sad a stray gun volley from the audience ripped into his manhood. Peculiar way to die.

WILLIAM: Dying is riddled with peculiarities.

LILLIAN: Fortunate Master Ian stood rehearsed to join our troupe.

(LILLIAN exits.)

WILLIAM: We bring you a scene based loosely upon a prior author's work, *Julius Caesar.* I compassionately adapted that little known drama for you rambunctious cowboys in the audience.

(JOSH enters.)

JOSH: Master William? Have you seen Betsy?

WILLIAM: Elizabeth is positioned behind the curtain as should you be.

JOSH: I was writing a play of my own.

WILLIAM: Before most writers dare write, they train in classics more years than you have breathed.

JOSH: I shall take my position, sir.

(JOSH exits.)

WILLIAM: In tonight's performance of *Julius Crockett,* we learn that mighty Julius, mayor of Santa Fe, held onto firm control over the town elders.

(SAMUEL enters.)

SAMUEL: Are we rehearsing, Will, ole boy?

WILLIAM: Should you raise the curtain.

SAMUEL: There is nare a person positioned behind that curtain.

WILLIAM: Did you call—

SAMUEL: *(Yells.)* Places! Places everyone! Immediately places!

(SAMUEL exits.)

WILLIAM: In this scene we behold the slain body of Julius Crockett cast upon the barroom floor.

(ANNIE enters, wearing a flower in her hair.)

ANNIE: William? Is this flower not the loveliest?

WILLIAM: You festoon any flower, dearest Annie. Samuel announced, "places."

ANNIE: Did he? Pretty, pretty flower.

(ANNIE exits.)

WILLIAM: Bliss. The elders of Santa Fe, egregiously and cold bloodily assemble around noble Julius, his blood splattered upon his killers' felonious flesh.

(IAN enters.)

IAN: Pardon the intrusion, Master William, but did you settle upon swords or guns?

WILLIAM: This is not the Forum, Ian. It is a Santa Fe barroom. Guns.

IAN: Thank you graciously for your vision. I am recent to your prestigious troupe, but may I be of service with revisions?

WILLIAM: Young Joshua trumpeted he is eager to assist.

IAN: Indeed, he is eager.

WILLIAM: Alas, no revision required.

(IAN exits.)

3

WILLIAM: Amidst this tragedy, I perform Julius' devoted friend and confidant, Sheriff Tony, I humbly plead, my greatest role.

(MARGARET and BETSY stroll in, talking.)

MARGARET: So, there we were, Lady Macbeth, your grandfather, and I, standing-room-only eyes fixed upon us.
BETSY: Oh, Grandmama.
MARGARET: Unbeknownst to Lady Macbeth, one bare breast protruding for all to see.
BETSY: Oh dear.
WILLIAM: Good ladies? Places?
MARGARET: Places now, William?
WILLIAM: If it so pleases.
MARGARET: It so pleases. So, your grandfather averted his eyes, breaking character not one perceptible moment.

(MARGARET and BETSY exit.)

WILLIAM: Ladies and gentlemen, I give you the death and aftermath from Master William Bowlinggreen's *Julius Crockett.*

(WILLIAM exits as the curtains rise.)

(Cast members, except SAMUEL, gather with guns and swords pointed downward toward an imagined body. WILLIAM pokes his head through the back curtains.)

WILLIAM: Leave room here for my grand entrance. Begin!

(WILLIAM ducks behind the back curtain as SAMUEL hurriedly enters, still dressing.)

IAN: "*It is the best of times.*"
MARGARET: "*It is the worst of times.*"
JOSH: "It is the American Civil War."
MARGARET: *(To SAMUEL.)* Pssst.
SAMUEL: Oh. "*Far, foul, filthy* worse than any French Revolution."
ANNIE: "Here lies our once noble mayor ..." Samuel? Where is the body? I cannot perform without a body.
SAMUEL: Oh, beg pardon.

(SAMUEL hurries offstage and brings back a straw-stuffed body, far too small for an actual body, and lays it tenderly and caringly on the floor.)

ANNIE: Thank you. "Here lies our once noble mayor, smirched and dismantled of spirit."
SAMUEL: "Sante Fe Mayor Julius Crockett."
IAN: "It is we, who with imploding implements of death bespattered his sanguine ichor upon our guilt-ridden flesh."
MARGARET: *(Elbowing SAMUEL.)* Pssst.
SAMUEL: Oh. "I have blood upon my nose."
JOSH: "Elders of Santa Fe, what say we to Mayor Julius' wisest friend, Sheriff Tony?"
BETSY: "Winds of change demand that Sheriff Tony side with noble intentions."
IAN: "If Sheriff Tony be friend to Julius, be he not villain to us? Stand we stained in judgment?"
BETSY: "Sheriff Tony will clothe us in blame."
JOSH: "Sheriff Tony will expectorate ruthless revenge."
IAN: "Tony will reel reckless, foisting horror that suns and moons weep pestilence and curses."
SAMUEL: "Pray this not be so."
MARGARET: "Dead Apache corpses cast medicine wheels breathing death of four seasons, of four humors, of four

setting suns. Heed warning, Tony lies enmeshed with dark soul of yon warm corpse."

JOSH: "Then we be in grave danger."

SAMUEL: "In much, such much danger."

BETSY: "Hark. Upon saloon porch echo Sheriff Tony's footsteps."

(WILLIAM enters.)

WILLIAM: More room for my entrance. "What be this? Be this my mentor's shadow? Eyes play tricks of cruelty upon windows of mind."

LILLIAN: "Eyes are windows for tormented hearts."

JOSH: "Mayor Julius has lain for he be slain."

WILLIAM: More emotion, boy. Gush. "Slain?"

SAMUEL: *(Emotionless.)* "Spiritless, sir."

WILLIAM: Any emotion, Samuel. "This cannot be."

BETSY: "One cannot countermand what elders of Santa Fe ill fatedly rendered."

MARGARET: "How stand you, sir?"

WILLIAM: "My cognition stands in allegiance with the good intentioned, whilst my heart matches cold clotting vessels which once sustained my companion."

MARGARET: "Stand you with us, sir?"

WILLIAM: "What measure would satisfy doubt? Winds carry my words throughout lands of coyotes, scorpions, and Zuni."

ANNIE: "Zuni long took leave from ancestral lands."

(IAN pulls LILLIAN aside.)

IAN: "Cass? I beseech thee. Leak thoughts sheltered from listening judgments."

LILLIAN: "Here, by piano where bordello night songs stoked Julius' fiery appetites did I pledge for his favor."

IAN: "Sheriff Tony's heart aligns with that turning to dust. He be at home amongst shadows. Be not subsumed."

LILLIAN: "Aye, and yet, you and I broke bread and exchanged embraces with fallen Julius. Raised voice in hymn and rubbed shoulders seeking internal view. Our children crawled and walked together, exchanged passion clear as mesas in noon sun."

IAN: "Rumors!"

LILLIAN: "Rumors, truths, rumors. Truth by any other name is truth."

SAMUEL: When did William add that line?

MARGARET: Ssssh.

IAN: "Disquietude. You invite prattle from Sheriff Tony's lips to incite common people."

LILLIAN: "More danger in restricting than indulging."

IAN: "Face and gesture trump throat and tongue."

LILLIAN: "Let us comfort sorrow and win allegiance. *Tomorrow and tomorrow* will the *world be our stage.*"

WILLIAM: "Job found no comfort in words. Neither shall I. *To be alive, or not to be alive,* that is my question."

SAMUEL: *(Too loud to MARGARET.)* Blasphemous muck!

MARGARET: You'll bloody piss off William.

WILLIAM: God sakes, Samuel! We curtain up in three nights!

SAMUEL: Herds of drunken cowboys belching, shooting off adolescent fire arms. You mix it all up. *Julius Cesar, Hamlet.*

WILLIAM: Unadulterated Shakespeare is cryptic to mere cowpokes. That is why in *Randolph and Juliana* I have—

SAMUEL: *Romeo and Juliet!* Now *Randolph and Juliana.* Our progeny's posterity darkens.

WILLIAM: Confound it! Twenty-minute break!

LILLIAN: Thank you, dear.

WILLIAM: Samuel! To my dressing room!

SAMUEL: A moment, William. Let my feet revive.

7

(WILLIAM and LILLIAN exit as SAMUEL sits, drops tablets into a gigantic goblet, and rubs his feet.)

MARGARET: You have been cheeky again.
JOSH: Betsy? I am a tad unsteady with my lines. Might we practice our love scene?
BETSY: I have a headache.

(BETSY exits.)

IAN: Josh! I shall help you.
JOSH: *(Yells.)* Betsy!

(JOSH hurriedly exits after BETSY.)

IAN: Not on your nelly will Josh settle for her no.
ANNIE: Joshua takes after his father, never accepts no from a lady.
IAN: His father? And who was his father, if I may ask?
ANNIE: His father? A mystery.
IAN: Lady Lillian confided that you, Josh's kind aunt, rescued the boy from an impoverished orphanage.
ANNIE: Did she?
IAN: So, was Josh's father your brother, or was his mother your sister?
ANNIE: His father was not my brother. Excuse me, please.

(ANNIE exits.)

MARGARET: Piecing it together, are we, Ian?
IAN: Helping protect your granddaughter, Lady Parsons.
MARGARET: Betsy stands strong. Attend your own obstacles.
SAMUEL: Betsy has a fiery temper, echoes of her grandmother.

MARGARET: I'll have you know, I was a refined lady at Betsy's age. My late husband married me for my mannered public inclinations.

SAMUEL: And your private inclinations?

MARGARET: You best study your script before Master William demotes you to portraying that bundle of limp hay.

SAMUEL: I suppose I should go and prostrate myself for his sermon about "all the good" we do for impoverished cowpoke souls.

(SAMUEL exits, drinking from his goblet.)

MARGARET: Well, Ian, are you without complaints or demands?

IAN: I am privileged to grace the stage with noble talents such as yourself, Lady Parsons.

MARGARET: Your frequent felicitation draws suspicion. Before you joined our troupe, I believe you to have snatched purses and filched banks.

IAN: I taught elementary subjects to snobby children of wealth.

MARGARET: The name of the school?

IAN: Many schools, many places.

MARGARET: No sense in pretending to converse with you when I can enjoy memories of conversations of reverence.

IAN: Madame.

(IAN exits as BETSY enters.)

BETSY: Grandmama? Did you see which way Joshua went?

MARGARET: Toward the creek to pout with spurned heart.

BETSY: I have my career to consider.

MARGARET: Careers cannot warm your feet at night.

BETSY: Grandmama!

9

MARGARET: When I met your grandfather, he was a painter.

BETSY: An artist?!

MARGARET: A painter. Pub signs. Hotel signs. A theatre marquee. Shadowed me like a puppy with his tongue out.

BETSY: I bet you spurned him.

MARGARET: Relentlessly.

BETSY: So how did you ... you know?

MARGARET: Master Thomas Teaslip and Company needed one lady dancer and one stage manager. We lied we were impeccably qualified, and when Master Thomas inquired if we were married, your grandfather grabbed my hand beneath the table, squeezed it, and resounded, "Yes."

BETSY: He did not.

MARGARET: By two o'clock, a magistrate pronounced us "man and wife." By four o'clock, we were whisked away in a carriage to Northampton. By seven, we dined on beef stew and suet dumplings. By nine ... I shall inform you when you are older.

BETSY: That is scandalous.

MARGARET: Twenty-two years of warm feet. Josh is by the creek. Be overly cautious and you will end up with someone the likes of Master William. Someone who I am certain must have dreadfully cold feet.

BETSY: You are wicked and I love you the most in the world.

MARGARET: That will change. Now off with you.

BETSY: I do love you.

(BETSY exits.)

MARGARET: Ah, warm-feet memories abound.

(ANNIE enters.)

ANNIE: Lady Margaret? Did you see where Joshua went?

MARGARET: I sent Elizabeth to engage Joshua in match-making mischief.

ANNIE: Those two fight like brother and sister.

MARGARET: Young hearts evolving.

ANNIE: I hope they are rehearsing their *Randolph and Juliana* scene. I adore Master William's love scenes. If only Joshua were amorous as his father.

MARGARET: How late in our association you breathe story of Joshua's regretted father.

ANNIE: Joshua's father described himself as, "absorbed, blinded to those who would love him." He wrote that in a letter to me.

MARGARET: Joshua's father wrote a letter to you?

ANNIE: A man buried in work.

MARGARET: Working men deceptively appear to live. And Joshua's mother?

ANNIE: Her heart chilled for abandoning infant Joshua.

MARGARET: Desperate acts gnash at our souls. Our compassion should be abundant for that suffering woman ... wherever she is.

ANNIE: You have wisdom, Lady Margaret. I do not.

MARGARET: Romantic notions are lonely creatures. I instructed Elizabeth that with age it matters not so much who warms your feet as it does to have warm feet.

ANNIE: I have my warm quilt.

(SAMUEL enters.)

SAMUEL: And about what are the grand dames twaddling?

ANNIE: Our feet.

SAMUEL: Arthritis and gout. I possess plenty for all of us. Rain is coming soon.

ANNIE: I thought we were in a drought.

MARGARET: Samuel's feet are perpetually inaccurate as is his gossip.

SAMUEL: In time we shall see about both.

MARGARET: Did William chastise you properly?

SAMUEL: William knows not crafted verse from snake-oil pitches.

ANNIE: William works exhaustively on our programs.

SAMUEL: William laboriously dismantles texts, not to mention gross plagiarisms of contemporaries. Next thing we know, William will muddle *Macbeth* or *Hamlet* with "Genesis" or "Revelations."

(WILLIAM enters.)

WILLIAM: Our spirits seem rather festive following such debauchery of art.

MARGARET: William dear? Annie and I were wondering how the love scene between "young Randolph and his fair Juliana" is progressing?

WILLIAM: I feel stifled, stuck as to how to end it.

SAMUEL: Perhaps the two star-crossed lovers could die.

WILLIAM: A fresh possibility. And then perhaps ... Randolph and Juliana could spontaneously rise from the dead.

(SAMUEL sings "Onward Christian Soldiers" loudly as he exits.)

Curtain

Act One · Scene Two

JOSH, kneeling, stares at his reflection in a river as BETSY watches, hidden in shadows.

JOSH: Calm waters, you reveal what God on high gifted me.

(BETSY steps forward.)

BETSY: If you long admire your reflection, you will turn to stone.

JOSH: *(Startled.)* How long were you watching?

BETSY: Enough that I now know excessive amounts about boys and vanity.

JOSH: I much rather feast my eyes upon you.

BETSY: The vast difference between men and women.

JOSH: Tell me heaps more.

BETSY: It is a natural law of temperament.

JOSH: I looked everywhere for you.

BETSY: And you saw your reflection in the river and your quest for me concluded.

JOSH: You have drawn me. I am curious if changes in my heart fanfare on my face.

BETSY: Boy's hearts parade over their faces. Only we girls can see it.

JOSH: Tell me everything.

BETSY: About boy's faces?

JOSH: If you teach me about my face, you will teach me about your heart.

BETSY: Certainly not. My costume must be checked for holes, boy. I need look my best for opening night.

JOSH: I am not a boy.
BETSY: Should I call you, "Master Parker?"
JOSH: My proper name is, "Josh."
BETSY: "Joshua" is proper. "Josh" is familiar.

(JOSH examines BETSY'S costume, eventually brushing her hand with his hand.)

JOSH: *"If I profane with my unworthiest hand, this holy shrine, the gentle fine is this: my lips, two blushing pilgrims ready stand to smooth that rough touch with a tender kiss."*

(JOSH kisses BETSY'S hand.)

BETSY: What if Master William hears your ranting of Shakespeare's words?
JOSH: *"Have not saints, lips?"*
BETSY: If Grandmama saw you, she would seize. As different as chalk and cheese, I care about getting to heaven.
JOSH: *"Have not saints, lips?"*
BETSY: Yes, they have lips.
JOSH: *"Then let lips do what hands do.*
(He touches her cheek.)
"They pray."

(JOSH briefly kisses BETSY on the lips and exits.)

BETSY: Oh dear, my feet sweat from warmth.

Curtain

Act One · Scene Three

WILLIAM, SAMUEL, and MARGARET are on stage.

WILLIAM: Let us resume. Where are the children?

SAMUEL: Preparing their love scene down by the creek. Stirringly well I might add. I shall fetch them.

(SAMUEL exits.)

WILLIAM: Lady Margaret? I don't fancy one who meddles, but Elizabeth must be wary of that orphaned misfit.

MARGARET: Mind your tongue, William.

WILLIAM: Orphaned boys are toxically incorrigible.

MARGARET: Joshua is a charming lad.

WILLIAM: Joshua is determined to seize that which he has not earned.

MARGARET: Joshua has an ear for rhyme, for rhythm. As did you as a young man.

WILLIAM: Do not confuse my youthful appetite to connect to the universal muse with this silly boy's grandiosity.

MARGARET: Then we shall shelter this charming lad until his "grandiosity" blossoms into true greatness.

WILLIAM: "Charm will disarm," as I wrote in my newest scene.

MARGARET: As you also wrote, "With cold heart I depart."

(MARGARET exits.)

WILLIAM: "Heart … depart." Splendid line. Captures the essence of a Scottish sheep baron going mad.

(LILLIAN enters.)

LILLIAN: Talking to ourselves again, are we?

WILLIAM: Lillian, my britches are too tight in the waist.

LILLIAN: Again, love? Let us take a peep.

WILLIAM: I cannot bend in the execution scene.

LILLIAN: Do not want that, love. I can take out a stitch or two.

WILLIAM: Why do they fight me so?

LILLIAN: Your britches seem to shrink each time we feast.

WILLIAM: The cast members! Why do they fight me so?

LILLIAN: Do they?

WILLIAM: Every word. Every phrase. They spare me no *elbow room*.

LILLIAN: Perhaps they wish to share riches of your fertile mind.

WILLIAM: *Battalions of sorrows* are forced upon me until my aging mind blanks for original verse.

LILLIAN: Poor William. Before we bed down, I shall rub your ice-cold feet.

WILLIAM: And my shoulders, Lillian, my shoulders ache dreadfully.

LILLIAN: And our shoulders. By morning we shall be good as new. More room in our britches, our toes warm, and our spirits light enough to spring from idea to idea like a ... like a what, William?

WILLIAM: Like a hedgehog.

LILLIAN: Like a hedgehog, is it? You have an enchanting way with words, dear.

WILLIAM: You relish my phrases, Lilly. You never challenge.

LILLIAN: That is what you and I have, plays and phrases.

WILLIAM: Ah, the stage, but no son. No male heir to continue. A curse to follow me to my grave. I could put that into the next scene. "To my grave." No, "To thy grave." No, "All this to thy grave for want of a male heir." Quite original.

LILLIAN: "Hedgehogs."

WILLIAM: I think Samuel will be less cheeky after our talk.

LILLIAN: I am certain Samuel is thinking this very moment how fortunate he is for your guidance.

WILLIAM: Once I had difficulties in Memphis with a young lad—

LILLIAN: I beg your forgiveness, dear, but I must betake myself to the powder room for the tiniest of moments.

WILLIAM: I was midstream in story—

(LILLIAN exits.)

WILLIAM: Naturally. *Let the world slide.*

(JOSH enters.)

JOSH: Oh, Master William? Did you read my script? I like what I wrote.

WILLIAM: You, a novice, like it. But will audiences? Critics will eat you alive before your first posters are nailed. Seize discipline.

JOSH: Discipline, sir?

WILLIAM: Daily routines to connect to the cosmic muse, paying homage to what is greater than you. Even I, yes even I, young Joshua, have sat for hours in the still of night, waiting for something worthy to erupt, only to uncover I am barren.

JOSH: I find writing easy, unstoppable like a train barreling down—

WILLIAM: Blazing nonsense! Immature rhetoric gushes from your silly head like impulsive kisses you toss to saloon women.

JOSH: Writing resonates with my very being, Master William.

17

WILLIAM: You have not attained enough blessed birthdays to know what "being" is. Throw your heart out to its fullest, have it rejected so that you ponder in misery, unable to eat, unable to sleep, unable to drink, expulsing everything that approaches.

JOSH: One of my characters behaves so.

WILLIAM: One of your characters?! From what life experience, lad?

JOSH: From watching you, sir.

WILLIAM: I am not your puppet! Earn your own experiences!

JOSH: Surely, I cannot live every act and deed—

WILLIAM: You *must*. When I wrote that greatest scene in which the Scottish sheep baron loses his daughter, I drew upon loss of my own daughter, immersed in depths that I could realize only with pen.

JOSH: You had a daughter die, good sir?

WILLIAM: Lillian was feverous for a fortnight. Ah, twas nature's hangman's noose, the umbilical cord which strangled our delicate daughter's first breath. To this day, Lillian is buried in grief that rips away at her duty as a wife, *water locked in eternal frost.*

JOSH: I feel saddened for you, sir.

WILLIAM: Do not be saddened for me, Joshua. Experience life. Your pen will realize what you despairingly survive.

JOSH: I want to feel murder in my heart as evil rips away at my soul, feel the sweetness of angels, and then have them bloody battle one another.

WILLIAM: Ah ... there is your solution, boy. Draw from that dark cloud upon your horizon.

JOSH: I have no dark cloud, sir.

WILLIAM: Perhaps three winks of mischief with a group of strangers with whom you once associated?

JOSH: I once dinned and bedded down on the plains with four rangers.

WILLIAM: Ah. There it 'tis. I smelled it. Horse thieves.

JOSH: Horse thieves?

WILLIAM: I read somewhere, yes, I did. Two of the four were hanged.

JOSH: Are you confident it was the same rangers?

WILLIAM: Unspeakable actions befall the company of horse thieves.

JOSH: But I did nothing wrong, sir.

WILLIAM: Joshua, dear Joshua. People upon these godforsaken terraces are peculiarly wary of one another. They string up *long rows of miscellaneous criminals.*

JOSH: Hanging? But I knew not the ranger men. Master William, please sir, you must help me.

WILLIAM: Embrace your stirred emotions and ignite your writing, laddie. Seek the reality of mist and rain upon your cheek. Write, Joshua, write.

JOSH: Hanging?

WILLIAM: Joshua. Leave me. Write. Write 'til dawn.

JOSH: I shall, sir ... Hanging.

(JOSH exits.)

WILLIAM: That should stir the boy's talents. To my own writing ... A part for myself. And the elderly rancher Lear, Locklear, no, Othello, uh Orson says, "Summons my three daughters at once. I must divide my ranch amongst them, as long as they declare undying love for me." Glorious.

(IAN enters.)

IAN: Master William? I understand we shall soon play in Phoenix.

WILLIAM: Choice of sixteen saloons. After we haul our fraying bodies across a sun-burnt desert.

19

IAN: It must be vexing to negotiate travel accoutrements required for our noble troupe. May I offer my services, tired William?

WILLIAM: Indeed, I have grown flagging these past towns. With aging, self-reliance evolves into liability.

IAN: Allow me to relieve you of a few burdens.

WILLIAM: Young Joshua will ride ahead and procure rehearsal space. That lad has a fiery passion for theatre.

IAN: Much havoc is wreaked by youth.

WILLIAM: He remains beneath guarded eye.

IAN: This lad gratifies your illustrious vision.

WILLIAM: We must hold more of these talks, Ian. Grow better acquainted. We older thespians may learn from this boy's vivacity.

(WILLIAM exits.)

IAN: *(To audience.)* We learn unexpected lessons from this boy's vivacity.

Curtain

Act One · Scene Four

WILLIAM is sitting at a table drinking wine and reading a book as LILLIAN prepares their plates.

WILLIAM: I prefer salad after my main, Lilly.

LILLIAN: So bloody French of you, William.

WILLIAM: Despite our name change, dear, we are unalloyed Hungarian.

LILLIAN: We have endured copious name changes. I would think "Istvan Semmelweis and Company" would have peaked curiosity. Shakespeare by Hungarians.

WILLIAM: We do not perform Shakespeare, Lilly, we perform, Master William Bollinggreen the Third plays.

LILLIAN: Of course, dear.

WILLIAM: Had I a son, William the Fourth, he would propagate my plays.

LILLIAN: Yes, dear.

WILLIAM: You patronize me, Lilly.

LILLIAN: Yes, dear.

WILLIAM: Are you listening, woman?

LILLIAN: Am I ... of course, dear. More wine?

WILLIAM: You never disagree with me.

LILLIAN: I disagree with you this very moment. Now finish your very French salad.

WILLIAM: Why is it I pine for a son, Lilly, and you never express an iota of longing?

LILLIAN: I suppose ... God did not see fit to grant us a second chance. I accept his greater purpose.

WILLIAM: I reject God's greater purpose.

LILLIAN: What would you have me do? Steal a child? Snatch one from the market? Make a pact with the devil to implant a son in my withered womb?

WILLIAM: No need for hysteria.

LILLIAN: Twenty years you ranted and blamed. This moment your face blames.

WILLIAM: Hell lays claim for my having broached the topic.

LILLIAN: I should die and have you rid of me so you can impregnate the west with little Istvans.

WILLIAM: Little Williams. It would raise the intelligence of the west—

LILLIAN: Little Istvans would be reason for you to abandon my keep—

WILLIAM: Little Williams. I would never abandon you.

LILLIAN: If women are abandoned in this godforsaken land, they die with hint of winter.

WILLIAM: I would never abandon you.

LILLIAN: I prepare a nice salad for you, with amorous candle light and tomatoes fashioned into tiny hearts and animals.

WILLIAM: It makes the tomatoes dry out. No one else in the universe dines upon tomato animals.

LILLIAN: Tomato caricatures are my greatest creation.

WILLIAM: You are inspired, Lilly. Why this is *a dish fit for the gods*. Tiny tomatoes carved into little camels.

LILLIAN: Horses.

(LILLIAN exits.)

WILLIAM: *To die by inches.*

(WILLIAM pounds the table and exits, carrying the book.)

Curtain

Act One · Scene Five

JOSH is sitting on stage, writing as LILLIAN storms across stage and exits.

JOSH: Good day Lady ...

(WILLIAM enters, carrying book.)

JOSH: What ails Lady Bowlinggreen?
WILLIAM: Tomato horses with humps. What have you there?
JOSH: Now that I am tormented, I am compelled to write.
WILLIAM: Hand it here, boy.

(JOSH hands notes to WILLIAM.)

WILLIAM: *(Reading.)* ... Good ... good ... Ah, inspired connection to your suffering. Boffo.
JOSH: I suffer ... insufferably.
WILLIAM: Writing is a consuming mistress, like ships to sea that snatch one's imagination, carry one far from ordinary souls chained to shore.
JOSH: The winds fill our sails and carry us beyond dreams as we set it down in our captains' log books.
WILLIAM: Do not over indulge in ship metaphors. Know restraint.
JOSH: I imagine you taught heaps of great writers, sir.
WILLIAM: Legions.
JOSH: I will gladly pay you to teach me, sir.
WILLIAM: Money? In exchange for connection to the muse?
JOSH: I do not mean to degrade your God-given gifts.

23

WILLIAM: How could an impoverished actor possibly remunerate me?

JOSH: Odd jobs. Stables hire me quick enough.

WILLIAM: Large stables with the best of thoroughbreds? Ever run your hands over their fine velvet coats? What does it feel like, laddie?

JOSH: I presume like a horse.

WILLIAM: You claim to be a writer, but you say, "Like a horse." Like our show-wagon-plow horse, Rosencrantz?

JOSH: I never petted Rosencrantz, sir.

WILLIAM: This is a lesson about *life*! Do not presume a touch of the goddess of animals is comparable to the touch of smelly, shackled Rosencrantz. Release your mind to dream.

JOSH: You said that I should write from true experience—

WILLIAM: Silence! Master Bollinggreen's words are truths and lies simultaneously.

JOSH: Madness, sir.

WILLIAM: Harness madness and release it, a rhythm of encompassing and releasing. Encompassing and releasing. Encompassing and releasing.

JOSH: A dance, sir.

WILLIAM: On occasion, invent a new word or two.

JOSH: As do you, sir.

WILLIAM: Dance the tango on a tight rope suspended between heaven and earth.

(IAN enters, cautious to remain hidden as he eavesdrops.)

JOSH: I understand, sir.

WILLIAM: *Never, never* understand! Only critics believe they understand. Artists must never understand.

JOSH: Yes, sir.

WILLIAM: Now Joshua, here's a humdrum book I found uninteresting, but there are passages that may possibly aid a novice.

(WILLIAM hands the book to JOSH.)

JOSH: I shall treasure it always, sir.
(Reading.)
"Charles Dickens. *A Tale of Two Cities.*"
WILLIAM: New, struggling writer.
JOSH: *(Reading.)* "Every human creature is constituted to be that profound secret and mystery to every other."
WILLIAM: A rambling struggle of a book. What is significant, laddie, is that this beautifully-bound book is from me to you. Now off with you. Oh, and by the way, you can pay me each and every Thursday.
JOSH: Thank you, sir. I shall.

(JOSH exits as IAN steps forward from hiding.)

WILLIAM: Spying from the wings?
IAN: Contemplating what my character Lucius must be ruminating from the wings, imagining the slain body of his once noble leader.
WILLIAM: Oh, good. Carry on. Ah. Rehearsal time.

(WILLIAM exits.)

WILLIAM: *(Offstage.)* Positions everyone! Make haste!

(WILLIAM and remainder of cast enter.)

WILLIAM: No sense burning daylight. We open two nights hence.
SAMUEL: Which play?
MARGARET: *Julius Crocket.*

WILLIAM: How can one know one's lines if one does not know, "which play?"

LILLIAN: We are in place, dear.

WILLIAM: All to the good. Gentle ladies, scene fourteen.

(LILLIAN and ANNIE position themselves downstage.)

LILLIAN: "Who calls upon my sheep farm?"

ANNIE: "It is I, Slim, sent by the wealthy Scottish sheep baron rancher, Orson."

LILLIAN: *(Overly depressed.)* "What news?"

ANNIE: "If thou art of such unenthusiastic disposition, I can retreat until all is well."

LILLIAN: "My dampened disposition over my beloved brother slain by Apache does not dampen my feminine curiosities. I command thee, approach."

ANNIE: "Distance is safe for revealing my master's intentions."

LILLIAN: "Closeness is commended for interpreting innuendos of voice and gesture."

ANNIE: "I invest not, Lady Sheep Herdress."

WILLIAM: Stop, stop. "Lady Sheep Herdress?"

ANNIE: I cannot remember her name, William. You continually change the names.

WILLIAM: I create names of rhyme and rhythm to transcend, my dearest Annie Dumbstrum. Memorize. Do not extemporize. Continue.

ANNIE: "I invest not ..." So, what is her name?

WILLIAM: Olivia! Olivia!

ANNIE: Thank you. "I invest not, Lady Olivia."

LILLIAN: *(Aside.)* "I shall stay steadfast with Slim's every breath, for 'tis not the content of utterance, but his encasing passion."

(ANNIE studies a note for a moment.)

ANNIE: This paper is blank.

WILLIAM: *(Losing temper.)* What difference if the paper is blank?!

ANNIE: I did not memorize lines that I was going to read. I mean, what a waste.

WILLIAM: "What a waste?" "What a waste?" I cannot begin to tell you, "what a waste." We do not read on stage. Words spring fresh from our bosoms as we give birth to originality. Orson's passionate words undress, caress, make love.

LILLIAN: William! Modesty forbids.

WILLIAM: And you, Olivia, you see a handsome youthful man in Slim. He torches your fiery lust, this provocative, sensual, naughty rogue, a *lion among ladies.* Remember what I was once like?

LILLIAN: I shall forage through my imagination.

WILLIAM: You two wonders of femininity stay and rehearse. Live the words.

(All except LILLIAN and ANNIE move into upstage shadows and freeze in place.)

ANNIE: I am in love with this blank paper?

LILLIAN: Not paper, my dear, you love the man who wrote words upon that paper.

ANNIE: William?

LILLIAN: Orson.

ANNIE: William playing Orson.

LILLIAN: Orson's words of love are for me, Olivia. As you read, you must feel Orson's words are for you.

ANNIE: William's words.

LILLIAN: Your wild passion drives me to passion.

ANNIE: "*Hope springs eternal.*" William wrote that.

LILLIAN: He says. Shall we begin?

ANNIE: "Good Lady of the Ranch."

LILLIAN: Wait. Move closer, my dear.

ANNIE: Here?

LILLIAN: Closer.

ANNIE: I never stand so close, not even with men, well, not for some time.

LILLIAN: I am a woman and I believe you to be a fetching man.

ANNIE: That is wild!

LILLIAN: Think only of the man, whom you wish with all of your heart will love you.

ANNIE: William.

LILLIAN: I must think of the man I want to love me.

ANNIE: That is me, Slim. Or you could think of a man from early in your life.

LILLIAN: I shall, a man who faded upon me.

ANNIE: That is sad, Lilly. Should I move closer? Oh my, this is really close. Your foot is touching my foot.

LILLIAN: My foot has not touched another for some time.

ANNIE: Mine neither. "Good lady of the ranch."

(Lights shift to JOSH and WILLIAM upstage, dim on ANNIE and LILLIAN who silently rehearse in shadows.)

WILLIAM: So, Violet, disguises herself as a male sheep hand, Slim, to work for Orson and falls madly in love with Orson.

JOSH: Like Viola disguised as a man in Shakespeare's *Twelfth Night.*

WILLIAM: No, no, no. This story revealed itself as I observed surrounding sheep hands.

JOSH: I learn as I observe too, sir. One night by a campfire, spinning yarns with the four Texas Rangers I told you about, a story vaulted into my brain.

WILLIAM: "Vaulted" did it?

JOSH: One of the rangers was beyond elderly. Dusty and smelled of chew tobacco and old whiskey on his coat stained in coyote blood.

WILLIAM: Grisly.

JOSH: He boasted of saloon women, conquests from younger days. He was too elderly to actually ... you know.

WILLIAM: Tragedy of epic proportions.

JOSH: In every town he flirted with women of the night. Women beautiful of skin, never beautiful of heart. A bumping of hands or a weak smile skipped his heartbeat, kept the paling ranger alive.

WILLIAM: If your presumptions ring true, such story would be realized by masters. Such as—

JOSH: You confuse me.

WILLIAM: Your assumptions are, and I dare speak metaphorically, would be like my preposterously hiring an incompetent actress, who weeped inadequacies upon the stage, for purpose to enliven my own skin.

(ANNIE, with a flower in her hat, steps into the light as LILLIAN exits.)

ANNIE: Oh, Master William? Do you think this flower makes me look like a gentle school governess?

WILLIAM: My dearest, Angel Annie, in this scene you are disguised as Slim, a male sheep hand. Review costume matters with Madame Bowlinggreen.

ANNIE: I like to review my dress with you. Pretty, pretty flower.

WILLIAM: Are we ready to resume, golden angel?

(SAMUEL, BETSY, MARGARET, and IAN resume movement as full stage lights rise)

WILLIAM: And the grand dame of the stage? Where is she?

(LILLIAN enters.)

LILLIAN: Powdering my nose, dear.

WILLIAM: Perpetually powdering. If men could watch.

LILLIAN: We do not allow men to watch because men do not separate themselves from intentions unintended for them.

WILLIAM: Ah, but we dream. Scene fourteen. Resume.

(LILLIAN and ANNIE perform their scene with unabashed and scintillating passion, rising enormously beyond WILLIAM'S wishes and titillating him beyond comfort, almost shameless pornography.)

ANNIE: "Good lady of the ranch?"

LILLIAN: "Come close so I may taste seeds of message upon thy breath."

ANNIE: "I repeat, are you the good lady of the ranch?"

LILLIAN: "Closer and surrender words of servitude upon my drumming heart."

ANNIE: "Once more, are you the good lady of the ranch?"

LILLIAN: "Woo imagination with rhyme and verse."

ANNIE: "I speak words from one afar, who cannot look upon thy beauty and retain command of tongue."

LILLIAN: "And is your command corporal to your own lamentations?"

ANNIE: "My command is fueled by fiery pining of none but my master. I whisper penetrations of words to fill thee with—"

WILLIAM: Dear god, me ladies! You usurp my words, arouse demons.

LILLIAN: As you commanded.

WILLIAM: I did not direct riotous lust to erupt before our deprived cowhand audience.

ANNIE: I thought it was my best performance.

WILLIAM: I have not seen you seduce so wickedly since ... since—

LILLIAN: Since when, William? Since when did Annie so wickedly seduce?

WILLIAM: ... Good lord. It is tea time. Twenty-minute break.

SAMUEL: I was becoming quite aroused.

MARGARET: For shame, Samuel!

(All exit except IAN and LILLIAN.)

IAN: You appear ill at ease, Lady Lillian.

LILLIAN: My husband beholds no magic when I move heaven to stir his heart.

IAN: Look to the master's dreams.

LILLIAN: I am no longer privy to his dreams. I starve in this wilderness.

IAN: William engaged young Joshua as his pupil.

LILLIAN: Pupil?

IAN: Named Joshua as heir to his troupe.

LILLIAN: I am blamed all moments in life for not bearing him a son.

IAN: William finds focus in this youth. Connect with your husband by praising his apprentice. Embrace this lad and find entry into bond reserved between teacher and pupil, between father and son. Do not starve, Lady Lillian.

LILLIAN: You tease me with hope unknown.

(LILLIAN exits.)

(IAN discovers JOSH'S book.)

IAN: Ah, Mr. Charles Dickens.
(Reading.)
"It was the best of times, it was the worst of times, it was the age of wisdom, it was the age of foolishness." Dare I lay claim to this fine book to grace my mantle in

31

older years. Or perhaps, duty calls. Inform the master of the disciple's disregard for his gift. Oh, mischief be mine. Where are shaman and clever witchery when I pine for drama? Perhaps all road maps to heart and demise wait to be charted in play. Sleep well Master William and young Joshua. Destined roles await.

(*IAN exits.*)

Curtain

Act One · Scene Six

In bed, LILLIAN *is reading while* WILLIAM *is restless.*

WILLIAM: I am exhausted beyond repair. *What o'clock do you make it?*
LILLIAN: Why so restless?
WILLIAM: I believe it is time I relinquish, "Master William." "*Sir* William" has a nobler ring. Less space on a poster, on a marquis. Perhaps, "Dame Bowlinggreen" for balance.
LILLIAN: *(Preoccupied reading.)* Hm?
WILLIAM: You are deaf to my heart—What are you reading?
LILLIAN: *A Tale of Two Cities.* A Mr. Charles Dickens.
WILLIAM: Hm. I once knew a Charlie Dickerson.
LILLIAN: *(Reading.)* "It was the best of times. It was the worst of times." Read here.
WILLIAM: *(Reading.)* "It was the best" ... *Wo-ho! So-ho* then. This Mr. Dickerson has—
LILLIAN: Dickens.
WILLIAM: *Wretched pilferer.* Plagiarized my sacred art! Now, *put out the light.*
LILLIAN: Plagiarized? But you have yet to publish.
WILLIAM: All the worse. A shiver runs through my frame.
LILLIAN: Here. Your personal notes in the margins.
WILLIAM: *My blood ejaculates this vexed writer.*
LILLIAN: It was lying on my pillow. I accepted you must be confessing.
WILLIAM: Confessing?! Dispose of it before I am demoralized.
LILLIAN: Then who left this lovely book for me?

33

WILLIAM: One in league with robbers.

LILLIAN: Entrancing binding. I witnessed young Joshua with similar book.

WILLIAM: A hideous binding *bespattered with rustic mire.* My feet are cold.

LILLIAN: Loving Joshua.

WILLIAM: Lillian!

LILLIAN: Perhaps you can create a larger role for the boy.

(LILLIAN rubs WILLIAM'S feet.)

LILLIAN: Who can fathom how human flesh chills as do your feet?

WILLIAM: I think too much. Blood swirls around in my head, leaving none for my feet. Ah, that feels good. A tad more with the toes. Ah, yes.

LILLIAN: I do believe Joshua has your stage presence— when you were youthful.

WILLIAM: Joshua, Joshua, Joshua.

LILLIAN: And a larger role for Ian.

WILLIAM: Ian? A scarcity of talent. I toy with demoting him to a role as an inept ranch hand. "Diago." Hispanic-like name. Diago could expect Orson to appoint him as the head wrangler, but I overlook him, appoint a younger man.

LILLIAN: Cassio instead of Iago.

WILLIAM: Diago! Di-a-go. Inflicts murderous revenge, undermining my trust for the woman who worships me. Diago. Pure evil incarnate.

LILLIAN: Remember when we saw Lawrence Hamilton play Iago in *Othello*?

WILLIAM: Lillian! I am creating. Why distract me with non-sequitur events? You side with this boy over me.

LILLIAN: Had we a son, surely young Joshua would be he.

WILLIAM: You acquiesce to this leech's desire to inhume you.

LILLIAN: I am of great cheer. Let me massage your other icy foot.

WILLIAM: *A secret to the heart nearest it.*

LILLIAN: That is a good pumpkin. Do you feel warmer?

WILLIAM: *(Becoming aroused.)* Ah yes ... yes ... I have not been so inflamed in months. Ah ha! My amorous enlargement.

LILLIAN: William!

Curtain

Act One · Scene Seven

JOSH is on stage, pouting when IAN enters.

IAN: My lad. Instead of basking with morning radiance, you appear devoid.

JOSH: If a young man fell naively into the company of four rangers and it was later learned, those rangers borrowed a horse or two—

IAN: Horse thieves?!

JOSH: Sssh, Mr. Ian, please, sir.

IAN: *(Whispering.)* Horse thieves?

JOSH: What may be the fate of the naïve man— hypothetically for my play writing?

IAN: Oh, your writing. Then I need not spare gruesome detail. I need not omit vivid, grotesque perversities which befall the naive who associate with rogues defying high plains codes of justice.

JOSH: What befalls one, sir?

IAN: He is hanged. Hanged and quartered.

JOSH: I shall be ill.

IAN: Actually, hexagonalled, six directions. Arms two, legs two, head one, private anatomical—

JOSH: Greviously ill!

IAN: Do not write about such, lad. Protect audience sensitivities. It grows far worse. Tongues, livers, ants, vultures—

JOSH: No more images! Please sir.

IAN: If ever you seek counsel over private matters, call upon me. Oh drat.

JOSH: What sir?

IAN: I do not wish to dispel your ennobling of charitable Master William, but do avoid becoming his slave.

JOSH: What mean you, "slave?"

IAN: I confessed a minor indiscretion to Master William. In a wink, he seized power over me. Threatened to inform those who would obliterate me.

JOSH: What did you confess?

IAN: I worship the man, and yet, his impetuous mood swings will one day propel him to sacrifice me, as happened with tragic Nicholas.

JOSH: Master William adored Nicholas.

IAN: I was in the audience that fateful night a stray bullet barbarously ...

JOSH: ... Tore into his manhood?

IAN: Poor wronged gentleman.

JOSH: You knew Nicholas?

IAN: Like a brother. As he died, I pledged to actualize his thespian dreams.

JOSH: Did you witness who shot him?

IAN: I was so close that titanic explosive powder saturated my clothing, and yet strangely, I saw no one.

JOSH: But how was Master William involved?

IAN: Never speak to Master William of less than perfect traits you possess.

JOSH: But I made known to him of my association with the rangers.

IAN: God protect you.

JOSH: Will he turn me over to the law?

IAN: I pray not. Master William has a soft place in his heart for your "bold vivacity." He boasts about your "originality" as well as your passion for his concealed, coveted hero, Master Shakespeare. Promote your plays. Perhaps some flashy advertisements.

JOSH: I can be bolder about my writing. I can demonstrate greater passion for Master Shakespeare.

IAN: May the heavens infuse zest into your spirit. Elephantine advertisements.

JOSH: I shall immediately fashion such.

(JOSH exits.)

IAN: Eagerness. Vivacity.

(WILLIAM enters.)

IAN: Top of the morning, sir.

WILLIAM: I fear mornings. I am but a hollowed cask, emptied by wine-draining demons of the night.

IAN: Allow me to replenish your vats with cheer.

WILLIAM: Make despair leap from weighted shoulders.

IAN: Young Joshua thrives, a spectacle to behold. Last night, he disclosed to Lady Lillian, the virtue of his writing original plays over ... how did he put it? "Those who plagiarize the deceased."

WILLIAM: The bugger.

IAN: Lady Lillian ebulliently embraced the boy's "bold vivacity."

WILLIAM: *(To self.)* This explains her investigations of me.

IAN: The boy jubilantly presented a gift to his stage mother, a Charles Dicken's book I believe.

WILLIAM: My discharged book. Like a corpse scripting beneath its nailed coffin lid.

IAN: Lady Lillian and this boy, joyful as twin spirits.

WILLIAM: Lillian suspired for a son, one who would eclipse my talents, leaving her free to dominate me with incessant pampering. Tomato animals.

IAN: The fairer sex indeed comforts warriors into gentle lap dogs.

WILLIAM: Not this day!

(WILLIAM marches away.)

IAN: Good riddance, Master William.
(To audience.)
You in this arena. How much would you pay to witness bona fide love shatter, witness wrath rise from ashes of stolen souls, witness true death? Would you lift your eyes from drink? Play Cesar and turn thumbs downward? Sport shall amuse.

Curtain

End of Act One

Act Two - Scene One

Following a drum roll, WILLIAM steps before the curtain.

WILLIAM: Good evening ladies and gentlemen. Welcome to a delightful evening's divertissement—
(Yells.)
Plague sores, Lily! These britches strangle my belly!

(LILLIAN enters and examines WILLIAM'S pants.)

WILLIAM: We curtain up tomorrow tonight. I cannot breathe.
(Yells to wings.)
Samuel! Haul up the curtain!
LILLIAN: Such a fuss, dear. Hold still.
WILLIAM: My manhood is being mortally gripped.

(Curtain partially rises.)

WILLIAM: Samuel, you may be aged, but surely you can raise your flag beyond half mast.
LILLIAN: Such vulgarity, William.
WILLIAM: Of course I am vulgar. I am on the rack.

(JOSH yells as he runs across the stage and into the wings.)

JOSH: I shall help Samuel, sir.

LILLIAN: Princely, big-hearted lad.
WILLIAM: When he is seeking, yes.

LILLIAN: That boy adores you.
WILLIAM: You adore him. He adores you. Worship blossoms in bewildering venues.
LILLIAN: Silly child you are.

(Curtain rapidly rises.)

WILLIAM: And the neck of my shirt. My throat is pinched.

(WILLIAM follows LILLIAN offstage as JOSH and SAMUEL enter.)

SAMUEL: Thank you, laddie. Arthritis is most unkind. Once in New Orleans—damp place New Orleans, below sea level—We were executing a hanging scene with Bradley Potterdam. Scene seven. Bradley splendidly stepped off the podium, feet dangling, face turning purple. The audience was aghast. The curtains closed. I went to lower Bradley from hanging by his neck. Arthritis. Here in my elbows.
JOSH: Oh my word, Mr. Samuel.
SAMUEL: Sometimes in my knees and ankles. A bit of warm Scotch helps—
JOSH: What happened to Bradley Potterdam?
SAMUEL: Say what?
JOSH: To Mr. Potterdam, hanging by his neck?
SAMUEL: When?
JOSH: Scene seven?
SAMUEL: Scene seven. Oh. Thunderous applause.
JOSH: Did Mr. Bradley Potterdam die?
SAMUEL: Die? Oh, yes, Bradley. No. Bradley dropped to the boards. Decked me one dodgy punch.
JOSH: Thank goodness. I mean that he lived.
SAMUEL: I witnessed closer brushes with death. Once in Cleveland, I was holding a piano up by a rope—

(BETSY enters, interrupting.)

BETSY: Joshua. There you are.
JOSH: Betsy! I looked everywhere for you.
BETSY: I was strolling.
JOSH: Alone? In this savage town?
BETSY: Must I have you protect me wherever I wander?
SAMUEL: I must re-secure ropes for heavier scenery suspended above.

(SAMUEL exits.)

JOSH: *(Yelling to SAMUEL.)* Careful, good sir.
BETSY: Today must be your day to look after the world, Joshua Parker.
JOSH: Samuel has terrible arthritis, you know.
BETSY: And now you are a surgeon.
JOSH: His arthritis results in heavy things falling. Perhaps we should stand over here.

(JOSH re-positions BETSY.)

JOSH: Your grandmother boasted we performed the best love scene she has observed in some time.
BETSY: You pause too often. I fear I forgot a line.
JOSH: I look into your eyes, and I am lost—We can rehearse now.
BETSY: Now?!
JOSH: Now is splendid.
BETSY: Why splendid?
JOSH: We are both here, alone, thinking about the scene.
BETSY: We are alone, Joshua Parker, and you are thinking about the scene?
JOSH: About you in the scene, the way you stroke my hair when you think I am dead. The way you lick poison from my lips.

BETSY: The taste of Lady Margaret's blackberry concoction squeezed into poison bottles.

JOSH: Sweetness on your lips.

BETSY: We should rehearse the poison scene.

JOSH: I could rehearse the poison scene the remainder of my days.

(They hold hands but break apart as IAN enters.)

IAN: Good day, children.

JOSH: Oh, Master Ian. We were ... rehearsing our final scene.

IAN: Developing your characters?

BETSY: Our characters are developed, complete.

IAN: My, my, we are assured.

BETSY: How is your scene proceeding?

IAN: My shortened soliloquy?

JOSH: It was the best you have done so far.

IAN: I thank you, I am sure.

JOSH: Betsy and I were about to take a stroll.

(JOSH and BETSY exit.)

IAN: *(To self.)* Caution children. Companionship offers false security.

(ANNIE enters.)

ANNIE: As usual, I missed my nephew by seconds.

IAN: He will resist being captured by any other than young Elizabeth.

ANNIE: When I was Betsy's age, I was head over heels in love with a ... a person like Joshua.

IAN: Much like Joshua?

ANNIE: Theatre was his being.

IAN: I think of theatre as my being.

43

ANNIE: Yes, well ... I must check my makeup.

IAN: Stay a moment.

ANNIE: I should not.

IAN: Should not stay a moment?

ANNIE: Well, I feel—

IAN: A betrayal?

ANNIE: Pardon?

IAN: To have a private moment with someone other than one's intended, is rather a betrayal. Like eating an apple out of the hand of an enemy, like bedding down with the opposition.

ANNIE: Oh dear.

IAN: You know what fascinates me? We pray that we are watched.

ANNIE: We do?

IAN: Watched by our intended. Pray their eyes feast upon our every move. Pray that if we breathe too fast or our pulses skip a beat, they see.

ANNIE: They do see, do they not?

IAN: Sadly, only we see ourselves. Our intended others look elsewhere.

ANNIE: *(Sniffing.)* Surely he sees me, knows my heart is breaking.

IAN: My handkerchief?

(IAN offers his handkerchief, but ANNIE declines.)

ANNIE: Life is so wrongful.

IAN: What is wrongful, my dearest Annie, is that we fail to look back and see those who watch us.

ANNIE: I do not want to look back.

IAN: None of us does.

ANNIE: But I do not—

IAN: Care to know who watches you?

ANNIE: I must go.

IAN: Your makeup waits. How careless I detained you.

(ANNIE exits and BETSY enters.)

IAN: You look dispirited, lass.

BETSY: I want my final love scene with Randolph to be my mesmerizing masterstroke, my tour de force, my—

IAN: Designs have no bounds this evening.

BETSY: But I cannot rehearse. Joshua left to attend strangers' stables.

IAN: Ah, laying obstructions for we who dream.

BETSY: Who but I dream?

IAN: Dame Margaret Parsons approached me.

BETSY: Grandmama?

IAN: She dreams *for* you. She pleaded for me to launch an acting troupe grounded in the classics.

BETSY: Shakespeare?

IAN: Not so brazenly. We must whisper among these attending walls of Master William. He is sensitive. An unwell condition compelled by a tributeless past. My sympathies reach out to his inadequacies, and yet, responsibility requires we move beyond, launch a troupe dedicated to cultivation. Master Samuel Postewaite, Dame Margaret Parsons, yourself, myself.

BETSY: And Joshua?

IAN: Joshua is ... no delicate way to state this, "is shoveling horse excrement."

BETSY: To pay for acting lessons.

IAN: I offered free tutoring, but misguided Joshua depletes his coffers to assure Master William's silence.

BETSY: Joshua has nothing to hide.

IAN: Oh drat. Scuttlebutt does not agree with my complexion, and yet, an innocent girl as yourself should not stumble for lack of knowledge.

BETSY: What did Josh do?

IAN: Often, my child, misfortune catapults boys into unholy acts.

BETSY: He gave himself to another girl?

IAN: Not that impetuous impropriety, but another, far more grievous.

BETSY: Misplaced the basket I weaved for him?

IAN: *(Aside.)* Can I corrupt angelic naturalness?

BETSY: Oh please, I beg you.

IAN: I must not.

BETSY: You must.

IAN: If I must, I must. Horse thievery.

BETSY: Horse ... Josh works at a horse stable.

IAN: A malignant temptation.

BETSY: This is dreadful.

IAN: I would be consumed with guilt had I not sparked your wisdom.

BETSY: Josh and I declared our love.

IAN: Love and deceit, inseparable bedfellows.

BETSY: Then ... I shall forgive Joshua.

IAN: On a daily basis? For boys, deceit is habitual.

BETSY: You grew out of it, did you not?

IAN: God bless the nuns of South Boston. Dwithers. If only Joshua had not positioned himself in a stable.

BETSY: With horses.

IAN: A fox in a hen house.

BETSY: Heaps of horses.

IAN: A wolf in a sheep ... place for sheep.

BETSY: I shall not abandon Josh.

IAN: When we play San Francisco, handsome, wealthy young boys will throw themselves at your feet.

BETSY: San Francisco?

IAN: In two months.

BETSY: Two months?

IAN: Or one.

BETSY: One month is not so far away.

IAN: A blazing marquee, "Eliza-Beth Nes-Beth" ... *Romeo and Juliet* perhaps?

BETSY: No more *Randolph and Juliana?* But I do benefit from what I learned playing Juliana.

IAN: We all benefit from what we all learned from your playing Juliana.

BETSY: More than a one-night run?

IAN: More than a one-week run. The glow in your eyes, child. That child horse thief is fading. In a trice, he is vanished.

BETSY: But Josh is falling from my eyes into my heart. Only death could dislodge Josh from deep inside here.

IAN: Death?

BETSY: I must find Josh at once.

(BETSY exits.)

IAN: Why need clever when we have the tool of death.

(LILLIAN enters.)

LILLIAN: Oh Ian, I mended your breast plate.

IAN: We would all be shabby but for your dedication. Samuel renders me terrifically tattered when he stabs me in the chest.

LILLIAN: Samuel is indeed zealous in stabbing you.

IAN: And how are your wounds mending?

LILLIAN: I have no wounds.

IAN: I pray I am not out of line, Lady Lillian, but I overheard you say that you endured facial abrasions from Master William's portrayal of Othello to your Desdemona. Pardon me, Master William's Orson to your Dorothy, Dedra, Darlene ... whatever she is called.

LILLIAN: Not quite the same rhyme, is it?

IAN: I would never be one to criticize Master William openly.

LILLIAN: Openly? Not your fashion.

IAN: Speaking what hearts intend requires minimal musing.

LILLIAN: Disguising what minds intend requires minimal heart.

IAN: Men are rarely accused of having heart, unless considered deficient.

LILLIAN: Women are rarely accused of possessing thought, unless ordained evil.

IAN: Lady Lillian, how is it you and I so rarely speak?

LILLIAN: Perhaps, because I detest you.

IAN: Spoken from the heart, I am sure. Have I offended you?

LILLIAN: Your predatory disposition escapes none.

IAN: Annie?

LILLIAN: Ah, Annie. Complexities elude poor Annie. Her innocence spills forth like brief-lived mayflies drawn to courtship. Stay clear of that divine woman.

IAN: It is not I for whom she has eyes.

LILLIAN: She worships my husband unabashedly. It is innocent, I assure.

IAN: She claims Joshua as her nephew.

LILLIAN: They resemble.

IAN: How much Joshua must resemble the mother who abandoned him, to be rescued by an aunt with mother-like love, whilst his father remains masked amongst shadows.

LILLIAN: I have scores of costumes to repair.

IAN: Ah yes, costumes. They are everywhere, are they not?

(LILLIAN walks toward exit.)

IAN: The sheriff of Dodge City was dis-invited to our evening of entertainment.

LILLIAN: I beg your pardon.

IAN: The sheriff of Dodge City—

LILLIAN: I am not deaf, merely perplexed, as you are not scattered, merely calculating.

IAN: Master William chose to exclude the sheriff since the sheriff could deliver harm to young Joshua. A fatherly act.

LILLIAN: As you indicated to me, William adores that boy.

IAN: Like a father, amongst shadows.

(LILLIAN exits.)

IAN: Ian, you improve impressively by the hour. With no heart, comes absolute freedom. No guilt, no remorse, no predestined bondage. Since bestowing mankind with free will, I wonder if anyone else contemplates how lonely God has grown.

Curtain

Act Two · Scene Two

WILLIAM is examining his pants waist as LILLIAN enters.

WILLIAM: My britches fit more appropriately.

LILLIAN: They cannot be "appropriated" further. Perhaps you as author could write fewer feast scenes for you as Orson.

WILLIAM: Feasts are essential to the magnitude of Orson.

LILLIAN: Magnitude overflows Orson's britches.

WILLIAM: You are most unchristian whilst I am in poverty of comfort.

LILLIAN: Do you believe you starve alone?

WILLIAM: We curtain up tomorrow, Lilly. No distractions.

LILLIAN: Distractions? Have you performed a scene with Annie recently?

WILLIAM: I am the writer, I am the director. I am in all scenes with all actors.

LILLIAN: I immerse myself in scenes with Annie's deplorable acting and never until tonight, did I question, why did the great William Bollinggreen discharge a mediocre actress like Annie Dumbstrum for a year, and then eagerly welcome her back?

WILLIAM: Let us bed down early, replenish our souls.

LILLIAN: You carry on with young Joshua as if he were family.

WILLIAM: You begged me to promote the boy.

LILLIAN: I am defective in bearing you a son.

WILLIAM: I absolved you years ago. I take my oath on the two testaments.

LILLIAN: The garden scene I perform with Annie? I was awakened more robustly than in years.

WILLIAM: I penned it superbly.

LILLIAN: Annie came forth with tenderness, reverence of charity and grace.

WILLIAM: It was God's choice that intellect would not burden her revealing nature.

LILLIAN: When I confined myself during months of grief, scarcely cognizant of your coming and going, where did you seek refuge?

WILLIAM: The cold desert air draws us to sonorous slumber.

LILLIAN: Did you nestle in the arms of creativity, writing like a madman late into night?

WILLIAM: Let us have a glass of warm milk, climb beneath our Hungarian quilt.

LILLIAN: Did you feel abandoned while I was dead mirroring our deceased daughter? I returned to you with expanded spirit. But this boy, you embrace Annie's boy.

WILLIAM: Annie's nephew.

LILLIAN: As you cradle this feral lad, you mock my barren womb for all to witness.

WILLIAM: This waif means little to me.

LILLIAN: It is far more than I can bear.

WILLIAM: Joshua can be a bit dodgy, but he is capable.

LILLIAN: Do you not see? Joshua must leave us.

WILLIAM: This lad's eyes are tuned to the zenith.

LILLIAN: A hint of coercion?

WILLIAM: Annie would fritter away.

LILLIAN: It is little consequence to you that I am misspent. When the curtain falls tomorrow night, it must be Joshua's farewell.

WILLIAM: Joshua adores living in our theatre family.

LILLIAN: If any man governs devices to persuade, my dear, it is you.

WILLIAM: There is the uncanny item that young Joshua fears he could be hanged as a horse thief.

LILLIAN: My god, William.

WILLIAM: A bit of a tease I used to stir the lad's imagination. And yet, he seemed seriously taken in.

LILLIAN: I shall have no hand in such mischief.

(LILLIAN exits.)

WILLIAM: Ah, but women are *masters of men's fate.* The masked ball lingers amidst the musical beating of woman's heart. Poor Joshua, with spirit of a warrior's writing pen, you stand aligned for glowing. Your dreaming invites malice from strange residences.

Curtain

Act Two · Scene Three

LILLIAN enters to join MARGARET, already sitting.

LILLIAN: Lady Margaret? I hope the evening is not too late.
MARGARET: What a delight! Have a seat, dear.
LILLIAN: May I burden you about a personal matter?
MARGARET: It would be an honor. Betsy's mother, Regina, was about your age when smallpox took her from us. Twenty years this Friday.
LILLIAN: I am saddened.
MARGARET: No, no dear. I announced that because your presence plugs that hole in my heart. There is no bond on earth like that of mothers and daughters. And granddaughters.
LILLIAN: My mother died when I was five. I remember her cooking kidney beans in goulash over a fire, but little more. I have no daughter. Or son.
MARGARET: So, you invest in William.
LILLIAN: Obvious to all. We are so distant from our Budapest. Now, endless grasslands, cowboys, *English.*
MARGARET: Your English is lovely.
LILLIAN: William is my world. I would die in this sweeping wasteland should I lose him.
MARGARET: Should I command him to behave?
LILLIAN: *(Laughing.)* He is frightened of you.
MARGARET: Well he should. The sport is this. We frontier women rely upon one another—and upon God. Men miscalculate they are imperial, oblivious what mothers and daughters talk about. Our knowing. We ferry magic within. We do not reveal such to men with words. We inform with our eyes. Wizardry shines through.

53

Prompting even the strongest kings and pharaohs to submit.

LILLIAN: This is what mothers and daughters talk about?

MARGARET: Disguised. From now on, dear, you and I must talk daily. Like mother and daughter.

LILLIAN: I would cherish that.

MARGARET: Daily.

LILLIAN: We shall.

(LILLIAN exits.)

(As MARGARET searches for her balm, SAMUEL enters.)

MARGARET: Samuel? Have you seen where I misplaced my balm?

SAMUEL: Would that be your arthritic balm, or your dry scaly skin balm, or your balm for nonspecific octogenarian afflictions?

MARGARET: My lip balm, thank you. And how might your octogenarian afflictions be conducting themselves?

SAMUEL: With fervor. I have no robustness that my rheumatism cannot divide and conquer. I shall aptly demonstrate should you join me in repose this fair evening.

MARGARET: And do what, pray tell?

SAMUEL: Sleep. It is not yet that day of the year when I defy Priapus' curse upon my manhood. Ninety-three days and counting.

MARGARET: Saint Louis! Ah, yes. We do roll on month after month, cow town after cow town.

SAMUEL: You are fortunate to have Betsy for enduring companionship. I so miss remaining constant enough to create memories for my grandchildren.

MARGARET: So, Samuel dear, if I were to join you this fair evening, what production would I experience?

SAMUEL: First, we would stare up at the ceiling, as if gazing up into opera house mezzanines.

MARGARET: Very good.

SAMUEL: Snatch a glimpse of a royal family.

MARGARET: Blue-blooded royalty.

SAMUEL: Together, coordinate a slow closing of eyes, pulling red velvet curtains over our worlds.

MARGARET: Promising.

SAMUEL: In the dark, whisper our most delicious and sultry memories.

MARGARET: Does it get any better?

SAMUEL: Could it possibly?

MARGARET: Samuel? You know what frightens me? Forgetting my delicious and sultry intimate moments.

SAMUEL: You will never forget Colin.

MARGARET: Just the other day, I told Betsy all about her "grandfather." I not once spoke his name, because "Colin" was not on the tip of my tongue.

SAMUEL: Yesterday, or some day this year, I could not remember my age.

MARGARET: I labor to keep Colin alive in thought, down to the way he instructed me to hold my fork and knife. Then a stumble in my mind misbehaves. Can you hold your wife's memory?

SAMUEL: What's her name's memory?

MARGARET: Eleanor!

SAMUEL: Ah yes, Eleanor. For years I panicked to leave everything precisely as Eleanor left it. In later years, I panicked I would cease to close my eyes and see her face, smell her Parisian toiletries, feel her nibbles on my ears, hear her singing Schubert.

MARGARET: A lovely voice.

SAMUEL: I accept that memory will leave, because I know those moments, those delicious, sultry moments will exist eternally amongst cosmic debris and winds. Eleanor and I measured up.

MARGARET: As did Colin and I ... I think I shall kip down in my own abode.

SAMUEL: So shall I.

MARGARET: When I close my eyes ...

SAMUEL: ... I shall also be closing my eyes.

MARGARET: I love you Samuel Postwaite, husband of Eleanor Postwaite.

SAMUEL: I love you Margaret Parsons, wife of Colin Parsons. Goodnight.

(They kiss.)

Curtain

Act Two · Scene Four

JOSH places a large poster on a wall, "Joshua Parker presents Tribulations of a Horse Thief*."*

(WILLIAM enters.)

WILLIAM: Jaj istenem! That is one towering notice.
JOSH: For windows of bars and hotels.
WILLIAM: Your play is complete so much as to bid this gargantuan exhibition?
JOSH: I stare at my monumental play bill, imagine the design of my colossal marquis, and I am inspired.
WILLIAM: Perhaps if you riveted your ingenious proclamation to telegraph poles and courthouse walls, you would be further inspired.
JOSH: I shall do that, sir.
WILLIAM: Do you think me dickwitted? I perfected cajoling and conniving, but never did I dethrone those who nurture my appetites. You fly far too near the sun, boy.
JOSH: Have I offended you, kindest sir?
WILLIAM: You are obstreperous with my gentlest directions. Scene five, *Julius Crockett.* How many times did we rehearse?
JOSH: Twice.
WILLIAM: Do not be short with me. I instructed you to deliver the line, "Julius has lain for he be slain" with a bellowing gush of tears.
JOSH: I try to perform it in the manner Master Shakespeare would think—
WILLIAM: What did you say?
JOSH: I beg your pardon, sir.

WILLIAM: You afflict me with haunted tributes of another playwright?

JOSH: You are like a father to me and I think of William Shakespeare as a father to you. Your verses resonate so exactly.

WILLIAM: I need no horse thief to instruct me about what is and is not original.

JOSH: I did not intend to—

WILLIAM: I have collective grounds to invite the sheriff of Dodge City to tomorrow evening's performance.

JOSH: The sheriff will recognize me!

WILLIAM: And about the girl. Never have I seen such delicate flower fall on such dusty path. Keep your dreams, boy, but leave the girl alone.

(WILLIAM exits as JOSH collapses to the floor.)

(IAN enters.)

IAN: My lad, you occur with *cadaverous color.*

JOSH: Oh good Ian, I do not know where to turn.

IAN: Withhold hysterics until your death scene tomorrow evening, and then bowl over our audience.

JOSH: Master William is inviting the Sheriff of Dodge City. He is assuring I am arrested.

IAN: The man is surrendering you into the clutches of the law? He will probably invite bounty hunters as well. I fear poor William suffers from a temerity I often see among Hungarians who adopt British stage names.

JOSH: I cannot show my face for them to see.

IAN: Perhaps makeup or a mask?

JOSH: I cannot convey depth of character if I am masked. These eyes, these lips, this striking frown.

IAN: Youth. To have one's universe revolve about one's emotions.

JOSH: They will watch every move I make. When I drink fair Juliana's poison, I shall truly be wishing to die.

IAN: My boy! You laid the answer before us! Your untimely death.

JOSH: My death?!

IAN: Cunning, momentous, dramatic. Center stage.

JOSH: I do not wish to die, not even center stage.

IAN: A feigned death, my boy.

JOSH: As an actor, I feign death. Real death is a career of enormous brevity.

IAN: Augur persuasively. Poison.

JOSH: Poison is too much like … like death!

IAN: A potion that paralyzes, a potion that mocks death to the horror of sheriffs and bounty hunters, a potion that leaves no horse thief to be hunted. And later, you wake, refreshed.

JOSH: Such a potion lives?

IAN: Did not fair Juliet partake of such potion?

JOSH: How find I such?

IAN: I never travel without it.

(IAN presents a small bottle to JOSH.)

JOSH: *(Reading label.)* "Dean Durboville Medicine Man Elixir Deluxe."

IAN: Great grandfather's retired business—God rest his soul—I have an infinite amount of his discarded bottles. Our last earthly connection.

JOSH: Amazing you have this.

IAN: On occasion I require such potion when I am wrongly blamed. Listen carefully, lad. Foreshadow your death. Conduct yourself as if desperate to end all held sacred.

JOSH: I could give away all my belongings.

IAN: Breathtaking.

JOSH: Act unworthy, shamed, fouled, despairing.

IAN: Overplaying raises suspicion.

JOSH: You are a splendid mentor, sir.

IAN: I fancy that concept, mentoring you to your death.

JOSH: Do not scare me, Ian. When I am older like you, perhaps I can live in intensity.

IAN: Older? That would be nice. Let us think of tomorrow as your last glimpse of sun and moon.

JOSH: How can I ever thank you?

IAN: I do what I do ... because I can.

JOSH: Thank you, sir. I am off. Guilt, despair.

(JOSH exits.)

IAN: Was I so demonstrably vulnerable at that tender age? I think not.

(ANNIE enters.)

IAN: Lady Annie, you appear frantically mislaid.

ANNIE: I uh ... was ... have you seen Master William?

IAN: He is in the bedroom plotting with Lady Lillian.

ANNIE: Plotting?

IAN: Did I say plotting? I beg your condonation. I mean to say that Lady Lillian is deciding who should and should not stay in our newly configured company.

ANNIE: Some of us will be asked to leave?

IAN: I am naturally relieved of course not to be ... relieved.

ANNIE: How do you know this?

IAN: Lady Lillian frequently holds me in confidence when she issues dictums to Master William.

ANNIE: Master William speaks his mind as much as any man.

IAN: Precisely. And therein *lies the rub.*

ANNIE: Oh, one of William's lines.
   (Giggling with delight.)
   You stole William's line.

IAN: Let us focus on pressing matters.

ANNIE: "Focus. Clarity. Simplicity." Lady Lillian is teaching me that.

IAN: Well she should. Lady Lillian feels her husband is bewitched by young Joshua as you use young Joshua to fasten yourself to William's favor.

ANNIE: Josh brings joy to William.

IAN: Which undermines Lady Lillian's authority. But you alone behold William is a great man.

ANNIE: He is great.

IAN: If only your devotion were not thwarted by Lady Lillian.

ANNIE: She will never leave William. Whilst Lady Lillian was sick and absent, William shone like a majestic ... majesty.

IAN: Greatness unbound by mysterious love.

ANNIE: I was that mysterious love.

IAN: No! And yet I suspected such.

ANNIE: It is painful to cloak my love.

IAN: Admirably performed.

ANNIE: You must say nothing.

IAN: I relish in saying, "nothing."

ANNIE: What can we do?

(IAN holds out another small bottle.)

ANNIE: What is this?

IAN: I dare not say.

ANNIE: Not ...?

IAN: ... Yes.

ANNIE: How evil.

IAN: How necessary.

(ANNIE takes bottle from IAN.)

ANNIE: How necessary.

IAN: How evil.

ANNIE: Remember, you know nothing of this.

IAN: I stumble through life unknowing, undaunted, unfazed.

ANNIE: I envy your gentle ignorance ... Why do you carry this with you?

IAN: Other souls demand it for noble intentions beyond my capacity to grasp.

ANNIE: But if other souls need it—

IAN: I have more.

ANNIE: Sweet Ian, be off with you. We have a play to perform and wine goblets for ...

IAN: For ensuring our fates?

ANNIE: *(Laughing.)* Another of William's lines.

(IAN walks toward exit and pauses.)

IAN: If I depart first, Lady Annie, I cannot remain and deliver my soliloquy.

ANNIE: Oh. Allow me to go first.

(ANNIE exits.)

(IAN faces audience, pauses, opens his mouth to speak, but then halts.)

IAN: In such a moment, could any mortal possibly render a soliloquy? I think not.

(IAN exits.)

Curtain

Act Two · Scene Five

Several seconds of black and silence are followed by honky-tonk piano music with guns shooting and cowboys talking. Sounds fade into a drum roll and stage lights rise.

WILLIAM steps before the curtain.

WILLIAM: Ladies and gentlemen, I trust you enjoyed our installment of saloon theatre as we presented, *As You Hate It.* During intermission, we pray that none of you fine Dodge City citizens were mortally wounded during that unfettered gun volley. Godspeed. For tonight's second offering, we present my newest work, *Orson.* I play the role of the Scottish coal, steel, and sheep baron, Orson, a man of five and sixty years, who struggles with visions for *tomorrow and tomorrow.* Sir William Bollinggreen and Company proudly present, *Orson.*

(WILLIAM exits behind the curtain.)

(Throughout <u>Orson</u>, we can see a small table that is off the proper saloon stage.)

(The curtain rises unevenly, with all cast members, except SAMUEL, staring at it with suspense and concern. They peer up at the curtain before moving cautiously into position.)

(SAMUEL limps onto the saloon stage.)

(The curtain falls a bit and cast members gasp. SAMUEL motions all is well.)

SAMUEL: *(To audience.)* "Orson. Scene one. A sheep pasture outside Denver. It is the Ides of July."
WILLIAM: "Good people in this sheep pasture outside Denver, on this Ides of July, come forth and celebrate our fruitful season of sheep shearing."
ALL: "Hear, hear. Joy to all."
WILLIAM: "Tonight and hence forth this fortnight, make merriment with fine wine and lamb chops."
ALL: "Hear, hear. Joy to all."
ANNIE: "Indeed you are *every inch* a sheep baron. Long live Orson."
ALL: "Hear, hear. Long live Orson."
WILLIAM: "From depth of heart, disperse. Generate festivity and sport."

(All cast members pause, forgetting to exit.)

WILLIAM: *(Loud whisper.)* Disperse!

(All cast members exit into the stage wings except WILLIAM and LILLIAN.)

WILLIAM: "You are admirably chirpy this Ides of July."
LILLIAN: "Your coal mines prosper exceedingly, your steel mills mightily churn out trans-continental railroad cars, and your sheep shed fleece with immensity beyond calculation. Your House of Mellons has deliciously beaten the House of Carnegies in all areas of consequence."
WILLIAM: "In all but one realm, my loveliest Darlene."
LILLIAN: "Surely my dearest Orson, there can be no realm for which you are anything but wickedly momentous."

(*IAN, standing off to the side of the saloon stage, removes two wine chalices from a tray and places them on the floor. He places two new chalices on the tray and from a bottle, pours poison into them.*)

WILLIAM: "My delicate flower, my empire of coal, steel, and sheep has no apparent heir."

LILLIAN: "We have three of the loveliest daughters bestowed upon blessed mortals."

WILLIAM: "Our eldest is a shrew whom no man's ingenuity can haply tame."

LILLIAN: "Kate is a scolding dragon as was her maiden great aunt Cleopatra, extirpated by a bite of her pet rattlesnake."

WILLIAM: "At least we are blessed with our young, radiant Juliana. She has the ravishing presence of my family."

LILLIAN: "Ah, but in that stoutheartedness *lies the rub*. No man shall rule her, not even one who abetted her creation."

WILLIAM: "Blasphemy! She predicts and pacifies my every whim."

LILLIAN: "Juliana bewitches her father for her own means."

WILLIAM: "Fair Juliana and I immerse in a game as old as mothers towing lines with sons."

LILLIAN: "Be amused and enjoy your Ides of July."

WILLIAM: "Your quick concurrence and charm bid alarm."

LILLIAN: "Charm will disarm."

WILLIAM: "Laws of man painfully collide with laws of woman. Cataclysmic finality reveals what neither fathom. All this to thy grave for want of a male heir. I shall decree that each of my three daughters declare their love for me. Only then shall I divide my empire amongst them."

LILLIAN: "With pronouncement of the death bed, games plummet with sour turns."

WILLIAM: "Men have not the patience of women, for men have not the gift of time."

LILLIAN: "With cold infusing heart, I depart."

(LILLIAN exits.)

WILLIAM: "Curses, and yet, Darlene is the fairest I know. Her bonny breast pressed against my knightly chest expunges black humors. Her challenges catapult me into reflection. Her anchor into laws of nature reign over my lewd inclinations. She is my every thing without which I am lost, and yet I grow weak as dark angels bid me to eternal sleep."

(WILLIAM bows and exits as SAMUEL enters.)

SAMUEL: *(To audience.)* "*Orson.* Scene Two. A bedroom in the main ranch house prior to sun set."

(SAMUEL exits as MARGARET and BETSY enter.)

MARGARET: "Fair Juliana, what incites you to doll up before setting sun on this Ides of July?"

BETSY: "Have I need of joyous reason, foolhardy nurse in this bedroom in the main ranch house?"

MARGARET: "You eclipse matters of the heart from Master Orson and Lady Darlene, but not from one who bathed you and focused your temperament from wean to proper lady."

BETSY: "I am amused by this night of sheep-shearing."

MARGARET: "Dare I ask who was in attendance?"

BETSY: "Good riddance to your ill-fated assumptions."

(At the offstage table, ANNIE removes the two poisoned chalices from the tray and places them on the floor

near the original two chalices. She places her two new chalices on the tray and pours poison into them.)

MARGARET: "Fair Juliana, secrets are safe within my custodian chest."

BETSY: "Very well then, perhaps there was a young man."

MARGARET: "Hallelujah. I have lived for this day since drying your journey into life."

BETSY: "Do you pledge unflinching stealth?"

MARGARET: "I am privileged beyond all hankering to share your confidence."

BETSY: "We limitedly glanced at one another during the sheep-shearing contest."

MARGARET: "A common sheep shearer?"

BETSY: "It was both the shortest of glances and an eternity of fusing deeply as if we were bare with no wish to hide. If he rises, I rise. Oh divine nurse, I am consumed. I dare not let him know and yet he too staggered from our moment."

MARGARET: "One glance?"

BETSY: "Life breathes anew. We are intended."

MARGARET: "Delirious child, the lamb chops do not agree with your reckoning."

BETSY: "Creation harmonizes our hearts."

MARGARET: "A wee bit of cod-liver oil will remedy this round the bend journey."

BETSY: "I resist remedy, beneficent nurse."

MARGARET: "Pray tell the name of this unknowing instigator."

BETSY: "His name is music, verse, and religion to my very breath."

MARGARET: "Undoubtedly."

BETSY: "He hails from Pittsburgh! Randolph Carnegie!"

MARGARET: "Good lord in heaven. Your father would as much see you dead as to catch you in conversation with one from the House of Carnegie. I am certain this

Randolph Carnegie's father would battle before he permitted a member of the Mellon tribe to tread upon his station."

BETSY: "It is fated."

MARGARET: "It is forbidden."

BETSY: "A heart is not subject to whims of emperors of coal, steel, nor sheep."

MARGARET: "Ah, but by a father's heart."

BETSY: "Remain discreet. Have I your pledge?"

MARGARET: "Oh woe is me. *I am shy of being confidential on a short notice.*"

BETSY: "I command you, learn all to be learned about my love. Get you to it."

MARGARET: "Tribulations abound."

(MARGARET exits.)

BETSY: "Randolph. What is a name? Randolph Carnegie, were he called Randolph of the House of Mellon, so would I still love him with all my heart. *A violet by any other name would still be a violet.* And so Randolph of the House of Carnegie, by any name will ye be keeper of my passion."

(BETSY bows and exits as SAMUEL enters.)

SAMUEL: *(To audience.)* "*Orson.* Scene three. The master's library in the main ranch house."

(SAMUEL exits as IAN and MARGARET enter.)

IAN: "Dear nurse, you honor me as you seek counsel on delicate matters, here in the master's library of the main ranch house."

MARGARET: "Mr. Diago, I knew not where to turn."

IAN: "This Randolph of Carnegie was abandoned as a child and raised by his elderly aunt after she was jilted at the alter. To this very day in his aunt's dining room waits her web-covered wedding cake, singing unrequited love of decades past. But no matter which Carnegie raised Randolph, *there's a small choice in rotten crab apples.*"

(SAMUEL sits by the offstage table, sets his gigantic goblet on the tray, drops his medicine into it, starts to drink it, but is stopped when WILLIAM approaches.)

WILLIAM: Pssst!

(WILLIAM gestures for SAMUEL to hurry and make sounds.)

(SAMUEL places his giant goblet on the floor, stands, and makes lightning sounds with sheet metal.)

MARGARET: "Oh God in heaven warns. The Carnegies are *such stuff as nightmares are made.*"
IAN: "I shall contemplate and devise."
MARGARET: "God smile upon you, kind sir."

(MARGARET exits.)

IAN: "Young ladies delight in rescuing men with sad upbringings, torching maternal proclivity. Soon Juliana will be disowned and the sheep empire will be mine for the taking."

(WILLIAM enters.)

WILLIAM: "Ah Diago. I commend your model sheep-shearing leadership."

IAN: "I am confident you will promote me to head ranch hand."

WILLIAM: "Despite your magnanimous labor, 'tis *out of the question.* This very moment before, I appointed a younger ranch hand, Slim."

(ANNIE enters, dressed in manly fashion, but with a flower in her cap.)

ANNIE: "I beg your pardon, gentlemen, but I misplaced my shearing implements."

(ANNIE retrieves shears from table.)

ANNIE: "Continue, sirs."

(ANNIE exits.)

(JOSH approaches the offstage table, looks at his poison bottle, and then pours the contents into SAMUEL'S giant goblet on the floor. He refills his bottle with wine from a chalice on the floor and exits.)

IAN: "Slim? Slim presents so woman-like."

WILLIAM: "I sense a devotion from Slim that if men could be befooled by other men, Slim's befoolery would transcend love. *Pretty dimpled boy.*"

IAN: "In that case, I show you this."

WILLIAM: "A handkerchief? Be this the fine strawberry embroidered handkerchief I gave Darlene upon our blessed wedding night? How come you by this?"

IAN: "I pray to not entomb you in dissatisfaction, but evil eludes."

WILLIAM: "I command you. Enlighten."

IAN: "Lady Darlene gave your prized strawberry embroidered symbol of wedded love to the woman-like man you promoted to sway your coal, steel, and sheep empire."

WILLIAM: "Slim? I am heated as a *green-eyed monster* rises within."

IAN: "I too, am smitten by this *foregone conclusion*." I leave you to your own devises, fabulous fabricator of coal, steel, and sheep empires."

(IAN exits.)

WILLIAM: "This cannot be. I summoned Slim to deliver my letter of love as if he were my own lips"—as you saw earlier this week in *Thirteenth Night*—"to the woman I adore from afar, Olivia, possessed in beauty and owner of the second largest sheep ranch in the west. Did Slim seize my love? This strawberry embroidered handkerchief proves that my once good wife betrayed me. Oh, this Ides of July abducts me into sneering ruin. My coal, steel, and sheep empire means nothing without my dearest Olivia—Uh Darlene. What chicanery and craft await as death so ill-fatedly approaches?"

(WILLIAM bows and exits as SAMUEL enters.)

SAMUEL: *(To audience.)* "Orson. Scene four. A sheep pasture outside Denver. It is nighttime."

(SAMUEL exits as JOSH and BETSY enter.)

JOSH: "Juliana? Are you here in this glorious sheep pasture outside Denver?"

BETSY: "Randolph? Is that you my love? Randolph Carnegie in this sheep pasture at night time?"

JOSH: "Oh yes my love, Juliana Mellon."

(They embrace and kiss with JOSH groping BETSY.)

BETSY: "Hark, is that a lark in the dark?"
JOSH: "Or pray tell a nightingale in the dell."

(They embrace and kiss.)

(At the side stage table, ANNIE replaces the chalices on the tray with two chalices from the floor. She walks away, but then returns and replaces one chalice on the tray with one chalice from the floor. Being confused, she exchanges two chalices on the tray with two from the floor, and then again one from the floor with one on the tray, and then confused, she shakes her head no, and empties wine from two chalices on the floor into SAMUEL'S giant goblet and exits.)

(Meanwhile, MARGARET watched ANNIE exchanging wine chalices. She walks to the chalices, smells them, appears concerned, and walks away.)

BETSY: "Such praying hands."
JOSH: "Such sweet lips."
BETSY: "Such saintly lips."
JOSH: "Then let us pray like saints with lips and hands."

(They embrace and kiss.)

(SAMUEL enters.)

SAMUEL: "Friend Randolph."
JOSH: "Best young San Antonio friend Mercutiok."

(ANNIE enters.)

ANNIE: "Master's daughter, Juliana."

BETSY: "Father's head sheep herder, Slim."
ANNIE: "Carnegies!"

(ANNIE holds out a spear.)

SAMUEL: "Mellons!"

(SAMUEL holds out a tomahawk.)

JOSH: "Fight not. Fair Juliana and I swoon in love."
BETSY: "If truth be told, no greater love has ever disentangled imprisoning webs of contrary families than that of young Randolph and his fair Juliana."
ANNIE: "With one from the House of Carnegie?"
SAMUEL: "With a Mellon?"
ANNIE: "Who is this pygmy of man to diminish the Mellon dynasty? Should I run through this Lilliputian?"
SAMUEL: "I glorify the House of Mellon. Is melon not a fruit upon which royalty dine? Melon, a melody of succulent, mellifluous, honeyed tastes fit for king and queen. Melon, a melodious musicality of mellow relish tantalizing taste buds of nobility."
ANNIE: "Is the name Mellon to be bantered by ye common ranch hand?"

(ANNIE holds her spear to JOSH'S chest, leading SAMUEL to stand behind JOSH.)

SAMUEL: "This common ranch hand writhes in torment for want of the cloying juices of a virtuous melon."

(JOSH deflects ANNIE'S spear as he moves aside, but this causes the spear to strike SAMUEL in the chest.)

SAMUEL: "Ah! I am grazed. Mortally I fear. Dearest Randolph, you should not have moved aside so swiftly."

JOSH: "Dear friend Mercutiok, I meant thee no harm."

(JOSH must help aged SAMUEL to the floor.)

SAMUEL: "Fare thee well, gentle Randolph. And may *angelic choirs sing me to thy sleep.*"
JOSH: "No!"

(JOSH hits ANNIE with SAMUEL'S tomahawk.)

(ANNIE dramatically prolongs her dying.)

JOSH: "Oh God in heaven, what have I done? My temper fired up from hell as I have never known."
BETSY: "Slim! Father's master sheep herder! Randolph! Our matrimonial destiny be doomed."
JOSH: "The houses of Mellon and Carnegie will brawl and battle."
BETSY: "They will grapple like Kilkenny cats. You must hide until all is resolved. I shall go and allay suspicions. I wait for you in pregnant pause."

(BETSY exits as IAN enters.)

IAN: "What wounding calamity has transpired on this Ides of July?"
JOSH: "My well-wisher Mercutiok, has been slain."
IAN: "How grievous young Mercutiok is slain."
JOSH: "And your master sheep herder, Slim, died at the hand of my ill-tempered fervor. I shall be pursued and castigated."
IAN: "Unless of course, all thought thee dead."
JOSH: "Oh gentle friend of Juliana and Slim, how might such remarkable skullduggery come to light?"

(IAN pulls out a bottle.)

IAN: "This potion is reserved for such affliction. Drink and you shall sleep the pose of death, only to awake refreshed two days by and by."

JOSH: "Mr. Diago, you have a heart that is cunning as well as devoted."

IAN: "I do what the gods bless me to do."

JOSH: "Please tell fair Juliana that I only sleep to preserve our promised love. Tell her to seek me out in the Church of the Good Shepherd at midnight. Our love's fate is in your hands."

(JOSH exits with the bottle.)

IAN: "The souls of stars above shed no tears in anxious wait as more harm stirs amidst these foreshadowed fields of blood-soaked wool."

(IAN bows and exits as SAMUEL enters and sets the tray with two wine chalices onto the stage.)

SAMUEL: *(To audience.)* "*Orson.* Scene five. The master's bedroom. It is twelve midnight."

(SAMUEL exits as WILLIAM and LILLIAN enter.)

(WILLIAM begins strangling LILLIAN.)

WILLIAM: The clock doth herald twelve midnight.

LILLIAN: "Orson! I did thee no wrong here in the master bedroom."

(WILLIAM holds out the handkerchief.)

WILLIAM: "Messages of deceit rise at inopportune moments."

LILLIAN: "I mislaid your strawberry embroidered symbol of love scores of times and you strangled me not."

WILLIAM: "It was mislaid in the custody of Slim. What say you?"

LILLIAN: "I say, Slim strangely fancied my strawberry embroidered hanky."

WILLIAM: "Slim is mystifyingly peculiar in those ways women bay at odds with what is manly, and yet, Slim shears as can no other."

LILLIAN: "Providence has it, Slim is no more. *To be or to have been.*"

WILLIAM: "Bugger. How know you this?"

LILLIAN: "From tidings of your most obedient Diago."

WILLIAM: "Diago. Fine herder, Diago."

LILLIAN: "Mischief resides in Diago, stirring envy amongst all in his company."

WILLIAM: "Diago. Was I so oblivious?"

LILLIAN: "*Human creatures are profound secrets and mysteries to every other.* And so it 'tis in the House of Mellon. Diago allied with your uncle to kill your father so that your mother could wed your uncle and rule."

WILLIAM: "Heinous accusations befall men into madness."

(SAMUEL enters dressed as a ghost.)

SAMUEL: *(Wavering ghost voice.)* "Orson."

WILLIAM: "Who goes there?"

LILLIAN: "Madness. Now talk you to walls and open air."

SAMUEL: "I am the ghost of your father."

WILLIAM: "Father? I am vexed by demons."

LILLIAN: "Perhaps a chalice of wine and a night's slumber."

SAMUEL: "Pampering poppycock. Diago conspired with your flesh and blood to bring you down."

WILLIAM: "Now Diago plots to betake my delicate Darlene. He I should not have trusted. He smells of chew tobacco and old whiskey on his coat stained in coyote blood."

SAMUEL: "Neither was Diago born of woman, but *ripped from his mother's womb.*"

(SAMUEL exits, stumbling as he cannot see well in his ghost costume.)

LILLIAN: "Comfort mystic talk with this gift of wine."

WILLIAM: "*Too much of a good thing* disconsoles. Have thee taste before I."

LILLIAN: "Derive ye suspicions as one ill-used?"

WILLIAM: "One ill-used by gods who steal sleep, appetite, and passions. We have wine goblets to ensure our fates."

LILLIAN: "My wary empire builder of coal, steel, and sheep, I shall drink before you, proof of trust and devotion."

(LILLIAN lifts chalice to her lips and sniffs.)

LILLIAN: This does not smell like Margaret's blackberry concoction.

WILLIAM: Lillian! I mean, sweet Darlene, drink.

LILLIAN: William, uh Orson, perhaps later to drink. Perhaps now to ... sword fight.

WILLIAM: Sword fight?

(LILLIAN pulls the sword from WILLIAM'S belt and postures to fight, forcing WILLIAM to posture with the handkerchief to fight.)

(MARGARET enters, carrying two giant beer mugs containing wine.)

MARGARET: Uh, dearest, uh Orson and Darlene. I bring thee ... fresher wine ... familiar of blackberries.

WILLIAM: What in heavens? Uh ... Good nurse, nurse of Juliana.

MARGARET: I did this very night witness Slim exchange chalices, good sire. Slim knows little of wine.

LILLIAN: Annie knew I would drink first and she, he, Slim hath brought me this wine of death.

WILLIAM: Then drink not *milk of human evil*, dearest Darlene, but pray continue ye with scripted verse verses impromptu versed verses, and later we shall deal with Slim who is still departed, I pray.

MARGARET: I take leave, sir, madame.

(MARGARET exits with the two chalices.)

WILLIAM: Now, drink thee from this other ... *as good luck would have it* and be *merry as the night is long.*

LILLIAN: Yes, I shall ... Juliana's good nurse is truly good. Is she or isn't she? That now is my question.

WILLIAM: Oh good lord, Lilly, drink and move beyond.

LILLIAN: *(Sipping from giant beer mug.)* "So hath our misfortunes risen from dire effects of Mr. Diago."

WILLIAM: "I shall reveal if what you speak of Diago and the death of my father be true. When our jesters perform the House of Mellon play tonight, in which John Wilkes Booth conspires to assassinate President Lincoln, I shall perceptively observe Mr. Diago's face for betrayals of guilt. *The play's the thing.*"

LILLIAN: "And if Diago validates he is so wicked?"

WILLIAM: "*The wheel of irony shall come full circle.*"

LILLIAN: "With your blood at a boil, you will be justified in revenge upon all who betray, a red bath the likes of which the world has never beheld. Devise. With coldness of heart, I depart."

(LILLIAN exits.)

WILLIAM: "*Oh foul and filthy air.* Such an ignoble and wicked *piece of work is woman.*"

(WILLIAM bows and exits as SAMUEL enters.)

SAMUEL: *(To audience.)* "*Orson.* Scene six. The cellar of the Church of the Good Shepherd in Denver."

(SAMUEL exits as JOSH enters, carrying bottle IAN gave him.)

JOSH: "Here sit I in the cellar of the Church of the Good Shepherd in Denver with my potion. If Mr. Diago hath delivered my message, my sweet Juliana will know I merely sleep. Should paths not cross, she will think I journeyed into death."

(WILLIAM, MARGARET, and LILLIAN enter.)

WILLIAM: "Where stows scoundrel who doth filch love of my youngest?"

MARGARET: "Here in the cellar of the Church of the Good Shepherd, melancholic sir."

WILLIAM: "As do all depraved Carnegies, the boy hides in shadows of what is holy."

JOSH: Pray thee, approach no farther."

MARGARET: "Good lord, what cradles he in embrace?"

JOSH: "A poison so swift that hawks drop for niff of its vapors."

MARGARET: "Oh woe is me. Juliana will rightfully condemn my actions."

WILLIAM: "Silence, foolish nurse. This vain Carnegie's idle chatter folds for lack of valor."

(*JOSH kneels and holds up the bottle from* IAN.)

JOSH: "Observe actions driven by one entangled eternally with the fairest and sweetest offered by the House of Mellon."

(*SAMUEL enters out of concern.*)

JOSH: "On this night dark angels shatter innocent hearts, I drink vile venom so my body may reflect the stillness of my cheated passion."

(*JOSH stands, tosses Ian's bottle aside, and retrieves another bottle from his costume.*)

SAMUEL: That is not the bottle I laid out for you!
WILLIAM: (*Loud whisper.*) Samuel! Off the stage!
JOSH: Good audience, on this lamentable hour in Dodge City—
WILLIAM: From whence spring these unscripted words?
JOSH: Dear sheriffs, mayors, and bounty hunters—
WILLIAM: Dearest audience, forgive our regretted straying.
JOSH: It may be I for whom you search, but I assure you that I am innocent of horse thievery. I drink this poison not in fakery, but in sincerity, in final desperation.

(*JOSH drinks from bottle.*)

JOSH: Friends, family, and future audiences that never can be—

(*JOSH collapses.*)

SAMUEL: What scene is this? Who am I?

(*ANNIE, screaming, runs onto stage and cuddles JOSH.*)

ANNIE: Oh Josh! That potion was for another!

WILLIAM: "Young Randolph from the House of Carnegie is dead. Let shepherds everywhere venerate his bravery."

LILLIAN: William? I think young Joshua is poisoned.

WILLIAM: "Make haste to shelter fair Juliana."

(BETSY runs onto stage and clutches JOSH.)

BETSY: You cannot leave me!

WILLIAM: My oh my. Young Juliana learned four or five lines early of Randolph of Carnegie's death.

BETSY: Wake up!

(BETSY slaps JOSH'S face and then listens to his chest.)

BETSY: No! No! We need a doctor!
(Panicked, to audience.)
For God's sake, is there a doctor in the saloon?

ANNIE: This poison was intended for others, not you, poor lamb.

LILLIAN: Intended for whom? For me?

WILLIAM: Juliana and dead arisen Slim are with delirium.

BETSY: I cannot breathe.

(BETSY examines the bottle and licks it.)

BETSY: There is no drop for me. Perhaps a drop upon sweet lips to gift me.

(BETSY kisses JOSH.)

WILLIAM: Finally! On cue!

SAMUEL: They rehearsed this all week.

BETSY: Oh Josh. Your lips are warm. I die in this moment with you.

WILLIAM: "Wretched day for the houses of Mellon and Carnegie. Never was there a sadder story than that of young Randolph and his fair Juliana, youngest daughter of Orson." Psst. Samuel? Curtain.

SAMUEL: Now?

ANNIE: He's dead, William. Josh is dead. Our son is dead.

WILLIAM: What did you say, Annie?

LILLIAN: God have mercy.

WILLIAM: Our son, Annie?

BETSY: Someone do something! Josh?

WILLIAM: Annie? Josh is my son?

LILLIAN: How could you, William—Oh my god! That poison was intended for me. Annie tried to poison me.

WILLIAM: Madness. The play. Uh … Slim returned from death, fairest Juliana is encumbered with grief, the House of Mellon is—

ANNIE: Have you no heart, William? Our son Josh.

SAMUEL: Whatever this scene is, this is our finest performance.

MARGARET: Samuel? I believe young Joshua truly is dead.

SAMUEL: Ah no. Godspeed, lad.

MARGARET: Come, Samuel. Betsy? No more for us to do. Lilly?

(MARGARET leads SAMUEL and BETSY offstage.)

BETSY: *(As exiting.)* Grandmama, I cannot live without Josh.

MARGARET: *(As exiting.)* I know, poor child.

LILLIAN: Are you coming, William?

WILLIAM: He was my … he was my son, Annie?

ANNIE: Our son, William.

WILLIAM: I had a son, Lilly. A *flesh and blood* son.

LILLIAN: I have packing to do.

(LILLIAN exits.)

WILLIAM: You never told me, Angel Annie.
ANNIE: You could never leave Lilly. You never will. Goodbye, William.

(ANNIE exits.)

WILLIAM: But the stage, Annie? Lilly? The stage. It's what we are. When foolish life abandons us, the stage remains.

(WILLIAM kneels over JOSH.)

WILLIAM: Not so soon in life, lad. What did you see as you stood before these foot candles? I see chairs and faces, lanterns and whisky bottles. But this stage, this space was your bedroom to dream where you walked. No God almighty breathes if my son dies to teach me of my stupidity. Oh, but if clocks could run backwards, if rain could fall up to heaven. If poison could drain from lips to bottles. My son, Lilly. I had a son.

(WILLIAM stands and faces audience.)

WILLIAM: Oh. Uh ... Ladies and gentlemen of Dodge City. I hope you enjoyed Sir William Bollinggreen's *Orson.* Join us in the future for ... for ... Samuel? Our curtain call.

(SAMUEL enters.)

SAMUEL: Blast it. No one tells me anything.
(Yells.)
Everyone back onto stage!

83

(Offstage cast members, except IAN, enter reluctantly. They push one another, motioning to return to the stage, glaring at one another, some crying. They join hands at WILLIAM'S direction and bow.)

(Sounds of clapping and whistling from a cowboy audience.)

(All except JOSH bow, and then break line to reveal JOSH'S body. They extend hands to JOSH, motioning for the audience to clap for him. They rejoin hands for a final bow.)

(Drum roll and medicine-wagon-calliope music.)

(IAN, dressed in colorful medicine-show-like cape and hat, enters carrying SAMUEL'S giant goblet. He sets the goblet on the stage and gestures for the audience to cease applause.)

IAN: Ladies and gentlemen, before we depart, I congratulate Master ...
(Beneath breath.)
Now sir.
(Full volume.)
William on decades of successful entertainment. And I proudly announce the establishment of a new acting troupe, "Sir Ian Durboville and Company."

(IAN reveals his own large poster with his image and picks up the giant goblet.)

IAN: With yours truly, dedicated to performing the classics of Sir William Shakespeare. To my dear mentor, who is retiring, as is time, William Bowlinggreen.

(IAN smiles, toasts, and drinks from SAMUEL'S goblet.)

WILLIAM: Scoundrel! *"Cowards die many times before their deaths."*

(JOSH suddenly springs up from the floor.)

JOSH: Mr. Durboville, no! That giant chalice holds the potion you gave me for sleep.
BETSY: Josh, no. The sheriff and bounty hunters can see that you are alive.
WILLIAM: There never was horse thievery. I fabricated.
JOSH: Then I am not a hunted man?
WILLIAM: No, my son.

(WILLIAM hugs JOSH.)

(JOSH and BETSY kiss.)

(SAMUEL attempts to kiss MARGARET, who pushes him away.)

ANNIE: Dear Ian, that giant chalice is one into which I discarded the poison you gave me. I could not find it in my heart to follow through.
JOSH: Mother?

(JOSH walks to ANNIE and hugs her.)

SAMUEL: I do not care a brass farthing, but that giant chalice is *my* chalice. And I dissolved my gout tablets in it. Arsenic, you know.

(IAN picks up an animal skull from the stage, stares at it, clutches his throat, and falls.)

LILLIAN: Oh dear god.
SAMUEL: I know indisputably that was not in this morning's script.

(BETSY rushes to IAN.)

BETSY: Mr. Durboville? Oh no! Is there a doctor in the saloon?

(MARGARET pulls BETSY away.)

MARGARET: Do not make *much ado about nothing.*
WILLIAM: And now, if we please, our curtain call.
SAMUEL: Are we sure it is bloody over?
WILLIAM: The peacock has displayed his final tail.

(WILLIAM gestures to JOSH to take center stage.)

JOSH: Gentle ladies and gentle men of Dodge City, Sir William and Master Josh ... Bollinggreen and Company bid you, "adieu."
WILLIAM: Well done, son. Well done.

(All of cast except IAN hold hands and bow. They then point to IAN for his share of the applause. WILLIAM prods IAN'S motionless body with his foot and shrugs. All but IAN hold hands again for final bow. SAMUEL runs offstage. The curtain falls with uneven descent, frightening the cast to gasp.)

(And of course, a formal curtain call may occur.)

Final Curtain

About the Author

A native of the South, DC Fidler has combined a career in academic psychiatry and cultural psychiatry with a lifetime of playwriting, acting, directing, composing music, and teaching creative writing and the dramatic arts.

He studied theatre, writing, chemistry, medicine, and psychiatry at the University of North Carolina at Chapel Hill, where he served on the faculty. He later served on the faculty at West Virginia University, teaching cultural psychiatry, clinical psychiatry, and acting.

A licensed psychiatrist, DC Fidler has lived and worked with the Alutiiq tribe in Akhiok, Alaska; the Al Moqbali Bedouin tribe near Sohar, Oman; the Kalkadoon Aboriginal Tribe in the outback of Queensland, Australia; and the Te Tau Ihu Maori Tribes on the South Island of New Zealand.

He began his acting career in outdoor dramas, summer stock theatre, and local films and television at age ten. He has written scripts and composed music for over fifty medical educational videos at UNC-CH and WVU. He has written twenty plays that have been produced in various community theatres and universities across North Carolina, Virginia, Ohio, and West Virginia, as well as St. Louis, Sacramento, San Diago, Los Angeles, Boston, Chicago, and New York City.

He consulted and appeared in educational productions for HBO, ABC, and PBS and performed in numerous stage plays including: *Hope is the Thing with Feathers, Night of January 16th, Thieves' Carnival, Blood Wedding, Our Town, A Life in the Theatre,* and *Fool for Love.*

DC Fidler is a scriptwriter, film director, and medical consultant for educational films using professional actors to demonstrate mental health issues. In addition, he is an active member of the Dramatists Guild of America and the Charlotte Writers' Club.

Fidler previously chaired the Video Committee for the American Psychiatric Association and served as President of the Association for Academic Psychiatry. In 2003, he was inducted as a Fellow of the Royal College of Physicians of Ireland. He serves on the Arts and Humanities Committee for the Group for the Advancement of Psychiatry where he is co-producing a video series on the History of Psychiatry.

He is author of the textbook, *Psychiatry for Actors: Building a Character Using Psychiatric Principles,* and author of the novel, *Boogieban.*

Plays by DC Fidler
* Voices in the Woods
* Guilt by Association (With RJ Casey)
* Three Diaries
* Sir William Bowlinggreen and Company
* Shiraz
* Anniversary of Miss Nanette Pringle
* School Children Hiding Under Desks
* Grams
* Camp Uni
* Boogieban (Two-Actor Version)
* Boogieban (Seven-Actor Version)
* Ahulaqs
* Elk and Wolf (With Travis Teffner)
* Santee Delta (With Travis Teffner)
* Celtic Crossing
* Stone Touchin'
* Daugherty Park Merry-Go-Round
* La Dynastie
* Gyges Solution
* Begat

Short Plays by DC Fidler
* Persons
* Cruise
* Mobile to Where
* Oman Truce
* Second Amendment
* The Greek God Club
* Four X
* Microscopic Misconceptions
* Drone Guns
* Moon Bugs (With Travis Teffner)

Novels and Textbooks by DC Fidler
* Boogieban
* Psychiatry for Actors: Building a Character Using Psychiatric Principles

Musicals by DC Fidler
* Pied Piper (With Lauren Horacek)
* Healer Man
* Medicine Show

www.ingramcontent.com/pod-product-compliance
Lightning Source LLC
Chambersburg PA
CBHW071124260626

47162CB00006B/2449